"Briar, I need my glass," Rosethorn ordered. "And I want quiet, understood?"

"Yes, Lady," replied Alleypup.

Briar grinned—Rosethorn was always convincing—and took a velvet pouch from the workbag. Carefully he slid out its contents: a round lens four inches across, its edges bound in a metal band, fixed to a metal handle. He passed it to his teacher.

Rosethorn examined Flick, talking softly to her the entire time. At last the dedicate sat back, frowning. "When did you get sick, and how did this illness develop?"

Flick answered weakly. At last Rosethorn stood, holding the lens out for Briar to take. As he did, he saw that drops of sweat had formed like pearls on Rosethorn's pale skin....

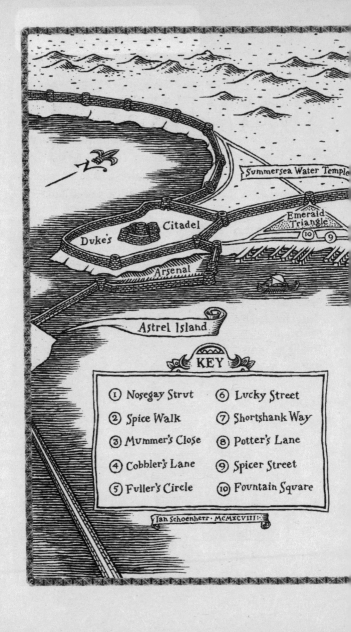

Summersea Water Temple

Emerald
Triangle
⑩ ⑨

Duke's   Citadel

Arsenal

Astrel Island

KEY

① Nosegay Strut   ⑥ Lucky Street

② Spice Walk   ⑦ Shortshank Way

③ Mummer's Close   ⑧ Potter's Lane

④ Cobbler's Lane   ⑨ Spicer Street

⑤ Fuller's Circle   ⑩ Fountain Square

Ian Schoenherr · MCMXCVIII

SUMMERSEA

Market Square

Copper
Triangle

⑧

East
District

⑦

⑥

④

⑤

② ①

③

The Mire

Urda's House

Fishing Village

Temporary
Hospital
Camp

Temple Road

Winding Circle Temple

POINT

TAMORA PIERCE
Circle of Magic

Briar's Book

SCHOLASTIC INC.

New York Toronto London Auckland Sydney
Mexico City New Delhi Hong Kong Buenos Aires

ISBN-13: 978-0-590-55411-4
ISBN-10: 0-590-55411-5

12 11 10 9 8 7 6 5 4 3   10 11 12/0

Printed in the U.S.A.   01

First Scholastic trade paperback printing, March 2000

The display type is set in Yolanda and Sophia.
The text type is set in Berling Roman.

Interior design by Cathy Bobak

ACKNOWLEDGMENTS

Thanks are due to my sister Kim, paramedic and nurse-to-be, for crash medical talks—any errors here in the descriptions of disease and treatment are strictly my own. Thanks also to my husband, Tim, for the encouragement and advice that saw me through a most worrisome first draft; and to Rick Robinson once again for all his help. Emelan and Summersea would not have their present shape, defenses, and currency without him.

I also owe a debt of research to books like William H. McNeill's *Plagues and Peoples*, Frederick F. Cartwright and Michael D. Biddiss's *Disease as History*, and Laurie Garrett's *The Coming Plague*, about the role that disease plays in human history and culture.

As I close this quartet, I would like to thank again the publishers who helped to see me through this bold new creative venture of mine, the editors and assistants at Scholastic Press here in the U.S. and at Scholastic Children's Books in the U.K. Between all of us, we have created books we can be quite proud of. Thanks also to my literary agents at Harold Ober Associates, always a safe port in any storm. My parents, Wayne and Mary Lou Pierce, supplied me with research as well as emotional support. To them and to Thomas Gansevoort, this series's creative godfather, I give my heartfelt gratitude.

$\textbf{B}$riar Moss knew he was only dreaming, but he didn't care. He sat in a giant oak tree, the heart of a great forest. A leather bag brimming with emeralds filled his lap, and the oak whispered the secrets of trees into his ears. He was running the gems through his fingers, admiring their color and size, when they evaporated. The tree vanished. Now two large, unkind-looking men in black leather hustled him down a wet, dark corridor. They shoved him into an open cell and slammed the thick door behind him. It boomed so loudly that it set up a string of echoes, each as loud as the first.

He opened his eyes. He was in the back of a wagon, tucked among an assortment of parcels and covered against the day's cold drizzle by an oiled canvas sheet. Something boomed repeatedly, like the cell door in his dream.

He thrust up the canvas to glare at the rider who kicked the wagon with such determination. "Leave off, Sandry!" he growled. "I was having the best dream ever and you woke me!"

Lady Sandrilene fa Toren, a girl of Briar's age, shrugged. The movement sent droplets rolling from her waterproof cloak and broad-brimmed hat. "Sorry." There was no trace of sorrow in her bright blue eyes.

"What's so important it couldn't wait, then?" Briar demanded. There was no use scolding her. Hard words rolled off Sandry the way rain poured off her cloak.

"I've been thinking," she said firmly. "Tris has a birthday—Daja has a birthday." She had named the other girls who lived with her and Briar. "I have one. That leaves you."

"You woke me to talk about *birthdays?*" he yelped.

"You said you don't remember yours—"

"I don't!"

"So pick one," Sandry ordered him. "It's not right, you having no birthday."

"I don't need one. What I need is sleep! Summer's coming, and that means weeding. I got to rest whilst I can, and you ain't helping."

2

She sighed sharply. Her pony looked at Briar with reproach in his eye, as though it were Briar's fault that Sandry bounced impatiently in the saddle. "Tell me you'll think about it, or I'll keep bothering you," the girl insisted.

She would, too. Sandry's determination awed Briar, though he would die rather than tell her that.

"I'll think about it," he said wearily. "Can I sleep now?"

"Why? We're almost to the Mire. I'll see you at home tonight." She clucked to her pony and trotted down the road.

Briar let the canvas drape fall and settled among the boxes and bundles. Birthdays! he thought. Only a girl-noble would think the day you came into the world was a thing to celebrate. His mother had certainly never mentioned it, that he could remember. Of course, he could just manage to remember her, a woman whose skin was as golden brown and hair as glossy black as his. She had smelled of cheap rose scent, and someone had knifed her one night as she came home from the inn where she worked. Briar thought he'd been about four then.

Memories like that were pointless. It was better to deal with his housemate: if Sandry wanted him to have a birthday, he'd better pick one and get it over with.

Briar yawned and shut his gray-green eyes. He wouldn't choose a birthday in *this* month, that was

3

certain. Even for Sap Moon, the weather was vile. Gusting winds tugged at Briar's cover. Icy rain pelted the cloth. Everyone who had pinned their hopes on an early spring now drooped as they went about their days. His birthday ought to be in a green month. That way he could plead garden chores to cut short any sloppy, sentimental parties like the one they'd had for Tris soon after the turning of the year.

The wagon's wheels lurched; its movement changed, making him slide across the many baskets and boxes that formed his seat. Briar went to the side of the wagon and peered out from under the drape. They had turned off Temple Road, the highway that ran between Summersea and the temple community of Winding Circle, where Briar, Sandry, and their housemates lived. Now the wagon clattered down Nosegay Strut, the main street of the slum called the Mire. Ahead Briar could see their destination, the large, forbidding, two-story building called Urda's House, where the city's poor came for the cheapest possible medical help. He wished that his teacher, the Earth Temple dedicate Rosethorn, didn't come here, but she took her vows to serve the poor seriously. He'd only once suggested that they stop bringing the medicines they made to this place. After she'd finished her answer, he decided never to bring it up again.

And why is it, he thought irritably, that every time we come here it's raining?

The wagon passed through the gate in the tall fence around Urda's House and stopped. Briar stood and began to fold back the canvas drape. As he did, he looked out through the gate, across the street. That winter he'd made friends with a girl named Flick, a thief of the breed called "street rat." Every market day that Briar came to Urda's House with Rosethorn, Flick met him there. Together they would roam Summersea, getting into things and swapping tales of Flick's days and Briar's life when he'd been a street rat in distant Hajra. Today, though, he saw no Flick, only a trio of street rats he knew to be friends of hers.

He hoped she wasn't in jail. He really liked Flick.

A woman in the dark green cloak and habit of one who had dedicated her life to the service of the earth-gods climbed down from the seat beside the driver of the cart. She thrust back the hood of her cloak to reveal a head of chestnut hair cropped mannishly short and parted on one side. Her face was lovely, with large, brown eyes, creamy skin, and a beautifully carved mouth. Briar had once thought she was her name, as pretty as a rose, as quick to bite as a thorn, before he'd scolded himself for romancing and shoved the notion out of his brain. Whatever else he thought, Rosethorn was a plant-mage, his teacher in the gardener's and herbalist's arts.

"Look alive, boy," she advised him crisply, coming to stand next to the bed of the wagon. "Those medicines won't do any good if they're wet."

"They ain't wet," he argued. "I wrapped 'em good." He handed one covered bushel basket out to her and another to the wagon's driver, who had come to help.

"Every time we bring you down here, all we've drummed into that thick skull on proper speech just gets buried in the mud," Rosethorn commented, shaking her head. "Stay up there—we'll do the carrying." She followed the driver up the steps to the wide porch and into the hospital.

It took three trips for the two adults to carry everything inside. Once that was done, Rosethorn took a final basket from the cart and thanked the driver. Briar hopped out. With a nod to the dedicate, the driver climbed onto his seat and drove away.

Rosethorn looked at Briar. "You're off to see that friend of yours?"

"If I can find her," replied Briar. "I didn't see her waiting."

Rosethorn pointed to a tower crowned by an immense clock, visible over the wall that kept city and Mire separate. "Meet me at the Guildhall at three o'clock," she told him firmly. "If you aren't there—"

"You'll hang me in the well," Briar said with a grin; it was a much-repeated threat.

"And don't stand here getting wet," she ordered. Shaking her head, Rosethorn walked into Urda's House. Briar crossed the street, inspecting the street rats as they shivered in the icy wind. Two walked

6

away, flicking their fingers at him in a casual wave. The third nodded.

Briar squinted. "Flick never told me your name."

"Alleypup." The other boy—smaller, dark-skinned and dark-eyed, dressed in tatters—shifted from foot to foot. He wore no shoes, only muddy rags wrapped around his feet. "Flick said I was t' bring ya."

"Bring me where?" Briar asked suspiciously.

"To her den, down below. She don't look so good."

"Don't look so good how?" Briar felt his own arms as if he warmed them. In truth he was checking that the hideout knives strapped to his wrists were in place, hilts set so he could free them quickly. There were other blades in sheaths all over his body, but the wrist knives were the quickest to reach.

Alleypup sighed. "She's got spots. You know, like she's sick. And she's got no coin for Urda. She asked, would you come have a look."

"Me?" Briar demanded, shocked. "I grow things— I'm no healer!"

"Flick told me, you seen sick folk before. You help Dedicate Rosethorn do up medicines and things. 'Course, if it's too much trouble—" Alleypup turned away.

Briar grabbed the street rat and glared at him. "I never said I *wouldn't*. I was just surprised, is all. Where's Flick?"

Alleypup led Briar into an open cellar and under

some lumber that leaned against its stones. Here was an open tunnel underground. A few steps inside brought them to a niche in the wall. The street rats had put oil lamps there.

"I don't s'pose you'd light these up?" asked Alleypup. "You bein' a mage and all."

"You want my mate Tris for that," Briar informed the other boy. In the language of the streets, a mate was the closest of friends. "Or Daja, that's back at Winding Circle. I can't do fire."

"Hmph," snorted Alleypup. "That's no help." He fumbled in his pocket and produced flint and steel to light the wick.

Briar's thin-bladed nose twitched as the reek of hot animal fat filled the air. He'd forgotten that scent—at home in the temple city of Winding Circle they used oil treated with herbs. The dog work of filling jars with oil and chopping herbs into them was his least favorite chore, but now it seemed the chore was worth some trouble.

And ain't I getting nice over such things in my elderliness! he thought as he followed Alleypup down the tunnel.

They crawled for about sixty yards. Splashing through a trickle of wet, Briar wondered how Rosethorn would react when he returned with mucky clothes. She was all too likely to dump him into a horse trough and keep him there until he was clean. Rosethorn liked dung as much as any gardener or plant, but she had strong feelings about it when it was on Briar. He was all too aware that this sense of being *dirty* marked another change in his life since he'd left the Hajran slums. Was he ever himself anymore?

His sense of direction told him they were headed west, under the wall that guarded Summersea proper. The network of clay pipes here sported cracks and leaks, the most recent damage from last summer's earthquake.

"Flick says you was street," his guide remarked, stopping for a quick rest.

"In Deadman's District in Hajra, in Sotat," Briar replied. "They called me Roach. I did purse and pocket work and burgled some."

Alleypup whistled softly. Thieves were important people—they had money once they'd managed to feed themselves. "How old were you?"

"Four." Briar stepped around what looked like a long-dead dog. "The Thief-Lord took me in after a while and gave me my name."

"The streets from four—that's harsh," Alleypup said, and coughed. Leaning away from Briar, he spat into the deeper running water of the city sewers. "My mum and dad only loped off two winters back. Said I was too hard to raise."

Briar slipped and had to brace himself against the walls around him to get his balance. Think I'll boil my hands afore I eat again, he thought. To Alleypup he said, "I never knew any but my ma, that died. Now I

9

guess my mates at Winding Circle, the girls, they're like sisters. They're complicated, though."

"Mages is always complicated," Alleypup commented. They had come to an intersection. He looked both ways, then led Briar right, into a larger tunnel. "We been hearing stories about you and them three girls since the quake."

They splashed on in silence for a while. The pipes got big enough that they could walk if they didn't mind hunching over and getting their heads knocked from time to time. These pipes were glazed clay, better in quality than the smaller ones, though Briar still noticed quake damage. Some of it had been repaired, the newer clay lighter in color than the old stuff.

Once they'd stopped for another rest—Briar noticed that Alleypup wheezed a great deal—the other boy remarked, "Flick says you was a jailbird."

"Have a look." Briar held both hands close to the lamp to let Alleypup see the dark blue X's tattooed between his forefingers and thumbs. "They grabbed me up a third time, and I was on my way to the docks," he said with pride. "But Niko—a teacher of mine—he saw my magic and bought me off the magistrate."

"Never!" whispered Alleypup, startled.

Briar nodded. "Truth. He brung me to Winding Circle. I ended up in a house with three girls because he saw the magic in all of us."

"Nobody saw you was magic before?" Alleypup

inquired. "All the time you hear about this kid and that one gets fingered by a magic-sniffer and bundled off for lessoning." Kid was street slang for a child. "And they're usually real little kids."

"Mine was strange," Briar replied with a shrug. "So was my mates' magics. *We* didn't even know we had it, till Niko and Lark and Rosethorn and Frostpine started teaching us. Lark and Rosethorn boss the house we live in. Frostpine's—"

"Metal-mage," said Alleypup. "Everyone knows him and Lark and Rosethorn." He straightened and led the way again.

At last they entered the great tunnels under the oldest parts of the city. More care and attention went into these underground rivers and streets, in part because the network was centuries old, but also because the guilds, the wealthy merchants, and those nobles who kept houses in town lived overhead. Here Briar was glad to see walkways on both sides of the stone- or brick-lined canals. There were rats, of course; the stink made his head spin; and often they had to race by pipes about to dump sewage into the water, but at least they weren't rubbing narrow walls covered with goo. These tunnels were built to last; what little earthquake damage they had suffered had been repaired with new brick and stone.

Not far from the point where they had entered the biggest tunnels, Alleypup turned into a lesser one. Ten yards down its length the street rats had yanked out bricks and dug into the earth, shaping a cave deep and broad enough to sleep a small gang. A lamp burned in a niche, casting a wavering glow over a pile of rags at the rear of the cave.

"It's me." Alleypup set his lamp on a ledge by the entrance. "I brung him."

The girl who lay on the pile of rags sat up, peering at them. "Briar?"

He walked over and knelt beside his friend. Except for a ragged belly-wrap of some pale cloth, Flick was naked. Her skin, normally deep brown, was covered with even darker spots and blotches from hairline to toes. Some on her left shin had merged into welts; they looked stretched and painful. Her lips cracked and bled; her eyes were glassy with fever. Heat rose from her to press Briar's face.

Flick struggled to smile. "Ain't I a sight?" She stretched out her hand, palm-up; Briar stroked it with his free hand. They locked their fingers together, twisted them, and tugged free in a traditional street-rat's greeting.

"You're something, all right," Briar admitted.

"I ain't never seen nothing like this—like these spots. Did you?" she asked.

Briar shook his head. "Open your mouth?"

She obeyed. Briar peered in, but the light was too chancy. "Alleypup, hold the lamp close."

The boy obeyed. Now Briar saw that Flick's tongue

12

was covered with a dense, pale coat. He could even see blue spots on the inside of her cheeks.

"Close up," he told her. "Lemme see your back." Obediently Flick turned onto her side. The spots were as thick on the back of her body as on the front. Asking permission and getting it, Briar lifted the band on her belly-wrap. The spots continued on the girl's hips and bottom. "You can lay flat again," he said when he was done. As Flick turned, he backed up until he was on level ground. There he sat on his heels, arms wrapped around his knees, to think.

For an apprentice maker of medicines, as Briar was now, his old life in Deadman's District had been useful. There he'd seen all manner of sickness and injury. Now he ran through those he had witnessed close up. Smallpox and all the other poxes were old enemies, as was the black death. They looked nothing like what riddled Flick's skin.

He looked at his friend. "How long've you been sick?"

She counted fingers, her lips moving. "Two days with spots. I wasn't feeling right three days before."

"Anybody else got it?" Briar asked.

Flick looked at Alleypup, who shook his head. "None as we know," Flick said. She didn't have to add, "Not yet." All of them knew that most speckled diseases were catching.

Briar stood. "I don't know what this is," he told

them. "I got to get Rosethorn down here." When their eyes went wide, he shook his head. "She hasta see for herself." He looked at Flick. "There's a closer route in, ain't there? If she came through the city, she could climb straight down to here?"

"You got to go to Urda's House anyway to tell her," Alleypup pointed out. "And they won't let me bring her through town. We'll get stopped at the gate." He pointed to his clothes, streaked with fresh muck.

"I'm going no place," Briar replied. "I got a quicker way to talk to Rosethorn than hiking back to the Mire."

"She won't come for no street rat," said Flick tiredly. "Nobody cares if we live or die."

"Shows what you know," Briar retorted. "Where do I ask her to come?"

Flick shook her head.

"Didn't I nick cough syrup for you back in Wolf Moon, that fixed you up?" demanded Briar. "Didn't I teach you how to throw a knife last time? I swear Rosethorn's all right. I *swear*."

Alleypup stripped off his filthy shirt and breeches, tossing them into a corner. The clothes he yanked from an open crate were somewhat cleaner. "Tell her meet me at the Guildhall clock." He pulled a worn tunic over his head.

Climbing the rags behind Flick, Briar pressed his hands to the raw earth at the rear of the cave. Even in the lamplight he could see roots hanging down. There were plants everywhere in the city. Digging his fingers into the rich dirt, he brushed a handful of rootlets, the beginnings of a vast underground web.

He and Rosethorn had thought of this over the winter. They could not speak mind-to-mind without touching, but they could talk through a web of plants. Closing his eyes, he found his magic, cool and firm with life. He passed it through his fingers, into the pale underground roots that had reached from the dirt to wrap around his hands.

His power split into a thousand small threads that flowed through grass and rose, ivy and moss, yew and cedar and ash roots. From one plant to another he sped, going in all directions except back. At the city wall he pulled himself together into a few dozen streams, plunging under the stone barrier to emerge in the tangle of weeds and poor men's trees of the Mire. He scrambled forward, Rosethorn now a blaze ahead of him, towering in his magical sight like a giant tree.

Ivy grew on the sides of Urda's House, framing the windows of the room where she worked. By the time he got there, she was opening the shutters.

This had better be good, she told him mind-to-mind as she gently wrapped her fingers in his vine-self. *I'm in no mood for jokes.*

He told her everything. When he was done, she untangled herself from the vine. He waited for her to reply, then realized she was gone, walking to the lower levels of the house. Just like her, not even to say

15

she's leaving, Briar thought. Letting go of the ivy, he raced back through roots again, falling into his own body. Only when he'd carefully freed himself of the roots in the wall did he try to speak to Flick and Alleypup. "Rosethorn. She's on her way."

"I'm off," said the other boy. He picked up one of the lamps and left.

Coming out from behind Flick, Briar noticed the water bucket and ladle. "Have you washed at all?" he asked.

She looked at him, feverish eyes scornful. "You think they let me in the city baths?" she wanted to know. "Dippin' my toesies with the draymen and the drunks? Did you think—"

Briar held up a hand, and Flick caught her breath. "Sorry," she mumbled. "I washed the first day of spots, before I got too tired. I'm weaker'n a kitten now."

Briar nodded. "Do you boil your water?"

"Why?" she demanded. "We get water from the Potter's Lane fountain. It's good enough."

"Even good water goes bad, 'specially if dung and pee leak into it." And I think maybe it is leaking in, Briar thought, but didn't say. "Maybe your water that ain't boiled is what got you sick."

"I had spots before I washed," Flick pointed out.

"So maybe you drank it." Briar could speak with confidence about this. One of his teachers had spent an entire winter's day talking about diseases in water. "You can't tell water's bad by looking."

"Wood and kettles cost money," growled Flick. "Don't yatter at me, Briar. My head's all swimmy."

"Sorry." Briar watched as she settled back, trying to get comfortable. Within minutes she was dozing.

He kept watch until he sensed Rosethorn's approach. "You took *forever*," he said when she and Alleypup walked into the cave. "I know turtles was quicker on the move."

Rosethorn's dark eyes took in the state of Briar's clothes; the corners of her mouth turned down. "That will be enough from you, my lad," she said. "This is our patient?" As she passed, she thrust her workbag into his hand.

Briar drew out a small, heavy pouch. Dumping its contents into one hand, he revealed a round crystal the size of his palm. Inside burned a steady, bright core of jagged light that put the smoking lamp to shame. He carried the light to a niche close to Flick and set it there. Its glare lit the street girl's spots cruelly. Rosethorn knelt beside her without a thought for her earth-green habit.

"Just hold still," she told Flick, her sharp voice gentle for once. "I try not to kill anyone who's already sick if I can help it."

Alleypup tugged on Briar's sleeve and pointed to the crystal lamp. "How'd you do that? Make it light up?" His eyes were hungry as they rested on the light.

"My mate Tris done it," said Briar, watching

17

Rosethorn in case she needed anything. "She put lightning in a crystal ball."

"Briar, I need my glass," Rosethorn ordered. "And I want quiet, understood?"

"Yes, Lady," replied Alleypup.

Briar grinned—Rosethorn was always convincing—and took a velvet pouch from the workbag. Carefully he slid out its contents: a round lens four inches across, its edges bound in a metal band, fixed to a metal handle. He passed it to his teacher.

Rosethorn examined Flick, talking softly to her the entire time. At last the dedicate sat back, frowning. "When did you get sick, and how did this illness develop?"

Flick answered weakly. At last Rosethorn stood, holding the lens out for Briar to take. As he did, he saw that drops of sweat had formed like pearls on Rosethorn's pale skin. For all that she acted calm, she was upset, as upset as she'd ever been when facing pirates or forest fires.

For a moment she was silent. Finally she straightened her shoulders and back. "This will take arranging, I think. Briar, I need you to link me to Niko—I assume he's at the duke's with the girls. Getting Flick to Urda's House will be tricky."

When Flick opened her mouth to protest, Rosethorn glared at her, fisted hands on hips. "Something for you?" she asked ominously.

Flick shook her head and sank back on her rags. Briar grinned: he'd known Flick was smart.

"Has anyone else been here since you first got sick?" asked Rosethorn.

"Just me, and I been out and about," said Alleypup. "Nickin' food and the like."

"We'll need to make a list of everyone you saw, then," Rosethorn murmured, thinking aloud. "Briar? Have the girls link us with Niko, please."

Briar closed his eyes as Rosethorn wrapped her hands around his. Unlike talking to Rosethorn at Urda's House, speaking to any of the girls was easy. He only had to look for them in his own mind.

Vedris IV, ruling Duke of Emelan, put down his empty teacup and smiled at his favorite great-niece. Lady Sandrilene fa Toren smiled back, glad that her visit had pleased him. The duke had passed a long, hard winter trying to repair the damage of last summer's earthquake, pirate attacks in the south, and a three-year drought in the north. Spring, with its promise of trade and new crops, was nearly come at last, and he could afford to relax with Sandry and her friends.

He didn't look worn down in the least, Sandry noticed. His brown eyes bore dark circles from too little sleep and the lines in his fleshy face were deeper, but his chin and jaw were still hard, his arched nose still proud. He dressed simply, but that was normal: her uncle was no fashion peacock. Vedris IV had no need to impress others with costly jewels and clothes. Instead he wore power and majesty like a cloak.

Sandry had changed from her riding clothes as soon as their group had reached Duke's Citadel. Now she was elegant, but only because she knew her uncle liked to see her dressed suitably for her rank now and then. Her gray, sleeveless overgown was beautifully woven and trimmed with black silk braid; her white silk undergown had silver embroidery on the flowing sleeves. Her brown hair, sun-streaked most of the year, was neatly combed, braided, and pinned under a gray silk veil. The quiet elegance of her appearance was countered by her vivid blue eyes and by the firm set of her round chin.

"More tea, Uncle?" she asked, reaching for the pot. "Niko? Tris?"

The steel-haired man on the balcony that opened onto the study shook his head, as did the chubby red-head seated atop the ladder that touched the highest of the room's bookshelves. The duke sighed and put down his cup. "I should see what Niko wants," he remarked, his elegant voice just loud enough to reach Sandry's ears. "I know it's trouble just from looking at him, and I had hoped for just one week with no bad news."

21

Sandry looked again at Niklaren Goldeye, the mage who had brought her, Briar, Tris, and their absent housemate, Daja, together. He was gazing at the city below. Niko's heavy black eyebrows were knit together over a craggy nose; the tight set of his lined face showed he was deeply worried. He had been like that for days. After over a year's friendship with him, Sandry knew the signs: he had read the future and seen dangerous events.

"I wish you could have gone without bad news, too, Uncle," she admitted.

The duke got to his feet. "Let's see from what direction this gale blows," he remarked, and went out onto the balcony.

Sandry looked up at Trisana Chandler. The redhead had found a book to interest her. Rather than climb down the ladder, she perched on it, her bespectacled nose close to the volume's open pages.

Someone—the duke or Niko—closed the balcony door. Sandry put down her teacup and went over to the ladder. "Tris," she whispered. "Tris!"

Her friend closed the book, using her finger as a bookmark, and peered at her, gray eyes vexed behind her spectacles. "There's no sense in asking me what's wrong. He didn't say, and I can't even guess. *I* can't see the future," Niko's student pointed out, her voice tart but quiet. "I was reading."

"You're *always* reading," retorted Sandry. "The only way people can ever talk to you is to interrupt."

"Then maybe they shouldn't talk to me," Tris said.

Sandry looked at her friend with exasperation. "What is it this time?" she asked. "History or biography?"

"Astronomy. Stars," replied Tris, stroking the book's leather cover. "The ones in the far south. They don't have the constellations that we have."

Sandry had suspected it would be a completely useless area of knowledge. Only Tris and Niko would care about the stars in a part of the world they might never visit.

At least she and her own teacher, Lark, had gotten Tris properly clothed for this visit to Duke's Citadel. It had taken them all winter to remake Tris's wardrobe of ugly skirts and dresses, partly because Tris had to be wheedled into fittings. The effort was worth it, thought Sandry. The rust-colored wool gown Tris wore today was embroidered with a pattern of green leaves at the collar and hem and fitted her plump frame perfectly. Normally Tris tucked her mass of wiry copper curls under a kerchief, but to visit the duke she had tied back her hair with a black velvet band.

Of course, color and flattering clothes could not soften Tris's face. Her stormy eyes were set in pale red lashes under fair brows and normally held the fierce look they did now. Brass-rimmed spectacles on her long nose glinted, as if lightning danced in the metal. Her chin was sharper than Sandry's, but no less firm.

23

"Do you think your uncle might lend this to me?" she asked now. "I'd take very good care of it."

"Ask him," replied Sandry. "He likes you."

"He does?" The redhead was baffled. "Why?"

"Niko sends him reports on how we do. Uncle said you're very clever. He told me you've worked hard to control your magic, and that's impressive in someone our age."

Tris blushed a fiery red. "We all work hard," she mumbled. She held the book down to Sandry and descended the ladder.

"Yes, but when *you* go wrong, everybody knows it," Sandry teased. "It's not a matter of a weaving flying apart, or—"

I want Niko right now. Rosethorn's sharp voice spoke deep inside their minds, from the place where they drew their magic.

When she sounded that curt, it was time to do as they were told. Both girls raced for the balcony door and pulled it open.

"Excuse us, Uncle," Sandry announced, walking out onto the rain-swept stone.

The men turned, frowning. "We needed to speak without interruption," the duke informed them.

Tris curtsied shyly. "It's Rosethorn, your grace," she explained. "She's talking to us through our magic, and she wants Niko. We don't dare say no."

The duke raised his eyebrows. "Who am I to argue with Dedicate Rosethorn?"

24

Tell him I'm sorry, Rosethorn ordered in mind-speech. *Say it can't be helped.*

Sandry and Tris obeyed.

Niko sighed, and lay a hand on Tris's arm. *Rosethorn, what is it?* Now that he was in contact with the girl, he could speak to Rosethorn as easily as if she stood beside him. Sandry remained, listening to the conversation through her own magical ties to Briar.

Have you ever seen this? Rosethorn asked. They all looked at Flick through Briar's eyes.

Sandry felt dizzy. Any disease that showed pock-marks reminded her of the epidemic that had killed her family. She stared at Flick queasily as Niko and Rosethorn spoke. Rosethorn was giving Niko instructions and a list of supplies. Why was oiled cloth so important? Why did Rosethorn tell Niko to bring herbs and liquids from Winding Circle?

Briar is in the sewers! thought Tris to herself, her skin prickling. Only Niko's bony hand kept her in place. Briar and Rosethorn and street rats, no better than animals themselves, in the worst kind of filth: the thought made her stomach roll. She hoped—she *prayed*—that Briar and Rosethorn would burn their clothes before they came home.

We won't be coming home, Rosethorn said. She had finished her talk with Niko in time to hear Tris's last thought. *Not for a while.*

Quarantine, Briar added glumly. *I knew it. We're to be cribbed up till we die or whatever.* He sounded like the thief he'd been when Tris had first met him.

But aren't there spells you can work? Sandry asked Niko unhappily. The four younger mages hadn't been separated overnight since they had first met almost a year before. *Spells that let healers see if people are sick or not?*

I don't think there are diagnosis-spells for this, Niko replied through their magic. *It's like nothing I've ever seen. We need time to watch how it develops.*

Time to prepare, added Rosethorn.

I must speak with the duke, Niko told her. *Expect me and those helping us at the Guildhall clock at—* He turned his head to look at the duke's own clock tower. *One. We should be there at one.*

Niko let go of Tris; Rosethorn did the same with Briar. *Coppercurls,* the boy continued, using his nickname for Tris, *bring my* shakkan *in tonight?* Briar loved his *shakkan,* a miniature pine tree, as much as he did their dog, Little Bear. *And close the shutters in Rosethorn's workshop? Tell Daja I'm sorry I didn't get the chance to buy that chunk of copper like she asked me to.*

I'll tell her, Tris promised.

It's my turn to feed Little Bear, added the boy. *And walk him.*

I'll do that. Will you be all right? Sandry wanted to know. The two girls could sense that Briar was nervous and upset. *How do you feel?*

Don't get quivery on me, Briar replied, trying to put cheer into his mental voice. *I'll have fun—den with folk like I'm used to, and not you sniffer skirts. Bye-bye, now!*

Tris, furious that he could joke, was about to reply angrily when Briar ended their connection. Sandry grabbed Tris by the arm. "Don't," she said aloud. "He just doesn't want us to know he's scared too." She looked around for Niko and the duke. They had gone inside and were talking urgently at the duke's writing desk.

"He didn't have to be mean," Tris muttered. "'Sniffer skirts' indeed!"

Sandry walked to the balcony rail and stared at the town below. Tris came to join her as rain began to fall.

"He's frightened," whispered the young noble, to herself as much as to her friend. "You could be nicer."

Tris growled, "You're always defending him."

"You're too hard on people," retorted Sandry. "You pay attention just to words, not how they're said. Briar's like you—he talks meaner than he is, and people fall for it. *You* should know better."

About to snap a reply, Tris saw the troubled look in her friend's blue eyes and changed her mind. She put an arm around Sandry's shoulders gingerly, half afraid Sandry might shrug off the contact. When the other girl leaned her head on Tris's plump shoulder, Tris relaxed. Without thinking she thrust the rain away, to leave them enclosed in a pillar of dry air. Both stood without speaking and watched as the weather cloaked the city.

* * *

When Rosethorn and the soldiers came to Flick's den, they found their way without a guide. "Your friend Alleypup ran when the duke's people climbed down the ladder," Rosethorn told Flick drily.

Briar and Flick eyed the soldiers, who wore long oilcloth robes and cotton masks on their mouths and noses. "I knew Alleypup was smart," the sick girl murmured. "He'da been locked up while you and your boy ran free."

"Not so smart, if he gives this to the people he runs into," Rosethorn replied as the soldiers eased Flick onto a litter.

"*You* may not care who else gets sick," snapped a guard. "He'll just scamper in the sewers, givin' it to them as works for a living—"

Rosethorn turned on him, dark eyes blazing. *"Not another word,"* she ordered.

The guard met her eyes and looked away. Briar could see the muscles of the man's jaw ripple as he clenched his teeth and held his tongue.

Rosethorn took a breath, making herself calm down. At last she shook her head and donned one of the spare oilcloth robes fetched by the guards. "We aren't running," she told Flick, handing a robe to Briar. "If this is catching, I won't risk spreading it. We go into quarantine with you."

The soldiers brought them out by way of a ladder that led up to a large grating in the market square. They lifted it to emerge inside one of the canvas tents used to cover sewer entrances when repairs were made underground. Now the tent hid them from the view of passersby. Someone had backed a covered wagon up to the flap.

They do this all the time, Briar thought, as the soldiers placed Flick's litter in the back of the wagon. They have the clothes already made up, and the wagon, and folk see the tent every day, so they don't guess there's sickness and run mad. His respect for the duke rose several notches. Twice he'd been caught in mob panic when the news got out that disease was in Hajra's slums. He'd escaped once to watch through sewer grates as people destroyed their own district out of fear of sickness. The second time, trying a bit of theft during the riot, had earned him a broken arm from a shopkeeper with a club.

He climbed into the wagon behind Rosethorn and settled into the corner. Rosethorn sat next to Flick, bracing her on the floor of the cart as they lurched forward.

Once they were moving, Rosethorn checked Flick's pulse and temperature. The street girl watched her and Briar, eyes glassy. "Willowbark tea, for a start," muttered Rosethorn, partly to herself and partly to Briar. "Why willowbark tea, student of mine?"

"To bring down the fever and make the ouches less," he said promptly. "Maybe aloe balm for her skin? I saw her scratching the bumps."

"Shouldn't I wash her first? Give me a suggestion,"

ordered Rosethorn. Noting the alarm in Flick's eyes, Rosethorn smiled reassuringly at her. "Yes, I said the bad word—'wash.' It won't hurt, not much. It didn't kill him." She jerked a thumb at Briar. "So it shouldn't kill you."

Flick grinned. Turning over on the litter, she began to doze.

When they reached Urda's House in the Mire, they entered the building through a back way built for quarantine: a separate, enclosed staircase with a gate that could be locked. The stair led to the third floor, which was empty when they arrived. Here the guards placed them in one of two large rooms just off the third-floor porch. Briar tried the inner door to the rest of the house and found it locked.

Examining his surroundings with a critical eye, he saw that it was well supplied. Deep, locked cupboards lined the two short walls from ceiling to floor, and cots lined the long walls. The shuttered windows were barred to keep unwilling guests inside. The only un-locked room that they might enter was the wash-room, set up with privies in cubicles, showers, troughs for washing clothes, and a great hearth in which a huge kettle of water steamed.

Flick got off her litter and sat on a cot, looking around. The guards spoke briefly to Rosethorn, then left. Briar listened as they first barred the outer door behind them, then walked into the second room that opened on the porch. He could hear them moving in the next room, settling in. He realized that in taking care of them the guards had already exposed themselves to disease and would have to place themselves in quarantine.

Going to the door that led outside, Briar opened a small speaking-window set in the wood at adult-eye level. It was covered by two lengths of finely woven sheer cloth, one fixed to the inside of the opening, the other to the outside. Both screens radiated a touch of magic. Holding his hand palm-out to the closer one, Briar found that someone had written magical figures on the cloth, the signs for health and purity. Smart, he thought. This way folk that're cooped up here can talk to outsiders without making them sick. He drifted over to the door that led to the inside of the house. It too had a smaller speaking-window, as well as a large sliding door set into the base. When he tried the sliding door, he found it locked from the other side.

"Bath time," said Rosethorn, gripping him by an ear and gently tugging him to his feet. "In there." She pointed to the washroom. "Get soap from the cupboards, wet down, lather up, stand under the grate, pull the rope. Clothes go into that." She pointed to a closed chute in the wall. "You'll find fresh new robes on the bench inside. Flick, I know you don't feel well, but cleaning up will help." She guided Flick to the other side of the partition that separated one of the rough overhead showers from the other.

Once he had scrubbed thoroughly and rinsed,

Briar found the new clothes Rosethorn had mentioned. The chief item was a loose garment like a robe secured by a cloth belt. He also found a fresh belly-wrap, a pair of gloves, and a cloth mask. Holding gloves and mask, he went into the main room and made a happy discovery: while they were washing, someone had slid food trays through the big lower flap on the door.

He carried the trays to a table. There were warm flatbreads, hardboiled eggs, and a pot of lentils stewed with onions and bay leaves. There was also a pitcher of fruit juice. Plates and eating utensils he found in a cupboard beside the table. He was just serving the food when Rosethorn and Flick emerged from the washroom, dressed as he was. They already wore their gloves, and their masks were tied around their necks.

"We got to wear this stuff?" Briar asked Rosethorn, pointing to his mask and gloves. "If we're to get these spots, we already got 'em, right?"

"Wrong. You wear them unless you're eating or drinking," Rosethorn told him firmly as Flick took a seat. "No arguments. And *please* stop talking as if we just dragged you out of jail."

Briar grinned at her and began to eat.

Flick ate a little and drank as much juice as Rosethorn could get into her. Then the sick girl went to bed. Already bored, Briar washed and dried the dishes. Rosethorn made willowbark tea. When it was ready, she woke Flick again. The girl protested drinking the bitter liquid but didn't have the energy to stand up to Rosethorn at her most insistent. Once Flick had sagged back onto her mattress, Rosethorn covered her, stood, and stretched.

Someone rapped on the door to the outer stair. The screened grate at adult-eye level slid open. "Rosethorn?" It was Niko.

Briar followed his teacher to the door. Standing close, the boy heard her quietly tell Niko, "You *knew*. You *knew* a plague was coming."

Niko's reply was a tart, "I didn't know much."

"You knew *something*. Green Man keep us, every *minute* healers get to prepare—"

"When you experience the absolute *welter* of bits and fragments that are the picture of time to come, you may scold. I only knew after midnight yesterday what we might face. *Might*." The sharp tone in his voice grew sharper. "I also saw fire and riot that may or may not happen, here or elsewhere around the Pebbled Sea—street fights and a rebellion against a king. Shall I take ship and warn every port that something bad will happen this spring?" His voice had risen. He caught himself and fell silent. Taking a breath, he added, "I got most of the things you requested here in the city. Your healer's oil must come from Winding Circle—why did you not have it with you?"

"I thought all I would be facing was winter colds and pains and a shortage of chilblain salve!" hissed

33

Rosethorn. "Not a brand-new disease! I should be working on a cure at Winding Circle right now!"

"That's *enough*," ordered Niko softly. "I am sorry I questioned you." He fell silent for a moment. When he spoke again, he did so in a whisper. "My dear, I admit that you will be needed desperately for your ability to unravel an illness and find its cure. Unfortunately, the gods placed you here. I know you dislike nursing above all things—but there is nothing we could have done to prevent it. Which do *you* think is more important: immediately isolating the few who were exposed to this child, or letting you go, possibly to bring infection to others?"

"Don't lecture me on the need for quarantine, Niko," Rosethorn snapped. "In case you've forgotten, I wrote the quarantine instructions for Summersea! I know I have to stay here!"

Niko sighed. "Have courage. There are other experts in this kind of work. I am sure that Dedicate Crane will find a way to identify the ailment and its cure."

"Yours is a happy nature," retorted the woman. "Crane will need help. With that lordly manner of his, I doubt he'll manage to keep anyone else for more than a day."

Niko shook his head. "You can't be that worried, if you can take the time to insult your colleagues. I'll come back with these things as soon as I can."

Frowning, Briar stepped back as Niko closed the grating and Rosethorn turned away from the door.

Somehow the boy had always known his teacher was uncomfortable with others. She seemed to like him well enough; she adored Lark, and enjoyed the company of Niko, Frostpine, and the duke. He even suspected she'd come to like the girls, but when it came to outsiders, she hid her softer nature and showed only thorns. Watching her handle Flick, he'd been surprised at how gentle she was. To hear she disliked working with people was no surprise. But Rosethorn was frightened?

That frightened *him*.

When the duke and his escort came to a halt at the gate of Discipline Cottage, a curly-haired dog two and a half feet tall at the shoulder burst out of the open door, barking wildly. Sandry and Tris dismounted with a splash, hurrying to get to their pet before he could terrify the horses. The soldiers grinned as the big dog raced around both girls, shrieking at the top of his lungs. Behind him came a tall, broad-shouldered girl with mahogany-colored skin—Daja Kisubo, another of Briar's housemates. Rather than go to tea with the duke or visit the market that day, she had chosen to stay home and assist her teacher Frostpine with a particularly complex piece of metalwork.

"How did it go?" Sandry called over the dog's noise.

"Fine," Daja shouted. She bore no sign of time spent in the forge, but wore a clean russet tunic and dark leggings. "The shield will be grand, once it's cleaned and polished." Her dozen braids were still wet from the bath; her round face was freshly scrubbed.

Out of patience at last, a scarlet-faced Tris yelled, "Little Bear, *down!*"

The dog Little Bear dropped to the ground and rolled onto his back, pawing the air.

"I'm not washing him this time," Daja informed Tris calmly.

"Young ladies," said the duke. The girls looked up at him. "Tell only Dedicate Lark what Rosethorn said—no one else. Once rumors get started . . ."

"We understand, Uncle," replied Sandry. Tris dipped a small curtsey. Daja looked from them to the duke, frowning.

"Aren't you coming in, your grace?" asked Lark from the cottage door. Like Rosethorn, she wore a green habit to show she served the gods of the earth. Unlike Rosethorn, Lark was tall and willowy, graceful rather than crisp. Her dark bronze face was catlike, with its small chin and wide cheekbones, and was framed with short-cropped black curls. The girls saw worry in her dark eyes as she glanced from them to their escort.

The duke shook his head. "I need to speak with Honored Moonstream on a matter of some importance. Good day to you, Dedicate." He bowed slightly in the saddle, then urged his horse forward. His guards followed.

"You're getting soaked, all of you," Lark said, watching the duke go. "Come inside. Where are Briar and Rosethorn and Niko?"

"In Summersea," replied Tris shortly as the girls passed Lark. Little Bear would have followed, but Lark shook her head at him.

"You stay and get wet some more," she told him firmly. "Rinse that mud out before you come in!" She closed the door in his face.

Once Sandry and Tris had shed their rain gear, they sat at the table with Lark and Daja. Sandry told them what she knew of the day's events. Tris watched Lark, not liking what she saw. The laugh lines around the woman's eyes and mouth had deepened; her lips were tight. She looked weary.

"I don't like this," Daja said quietly when Sandry had finished. "Not at all." Getting up, she went to the cottage's shrine in the corner by the front door. With a hand that trembled, she lit the candles for health and luck and set a pinch of incense to burn.

"I knew they had read omens for an epidemic," Lark commented, watching Daja. "Moonstream summoned the full temple council and all the healers while you were gone and told us. Ah, I was being silly." She scrubbed her face with her hands.

"Silly how?" asked Sandry, putting an arm around her teacher.

"It's been three years since our last epidemic. I'd hoped it might stay that way forever. I don't know how Crane's going to manage without Rosethorn," Lark said, getting up to make tea. "He'll say she got herself thrown into quarantine on purpose."

"What has Crane to do with anything?" Tris inquired. None of the young people at Discipline Cottage liked Crane, the mage who was also first, or head, dedicate of Winding Circle's Air Temple.

"He and Rosethorn are always set to finding the nature of any new illness and creating a remedy," explained Lark.

"He and Rosethorn *work* together?" asked Daja, shocked. "They *hate* each other."

"I didn't say they liked it," replied Lark with a tiny smile.

Little Bear crept in the back door, looking as meek as a thoroughly soaked large dog could look. His ears were down; his tail gave the tiniest of wags. Since the mud had been rinsed from his coat, no one told him to go. As Lark poured out tea, the dog trotted over to them. Something made him rock back on his haunches and whine deep in his throat.

"What?" Tris demanded, wiping her lenses with her handkerchief.

Little Bear circled the table, sniffing each girl. He whined again.

"You don't get fed until this evening," Daja said curtly.

The dog trotted into Briar's room; a moment later

they heard him whimper. Coming to the door of the main room, Little Bear barked sharply.

"Briar's not coming," Sandry told him, her mouth quivering. "Now stop it."

"I don't see how he can know Briar's not coming back," remarked Daja impatiently. Frightened by the other meaning of what she'd just said, she added hurriedly, "Not right away. He's not coming back *right away.*"

Sandry and Lark made the gods-circle on their chests.

Tris thrust herself away from the table so hard that she knocked over the bench on which she sat. Struggling to pick it up, she cried, "It's their own fault! What were they doing mucking about the Mire anyway? Everyone knows the poor breed disease!"

Sandry and Daja held their breath as Lark gazed soberly at Tris, raising her eyebrows. Even Tris knew she had gone too far. Her face was beet red with embarrassment and fury, but she met Lark's brown eyes squarely.

"If they could afford decent places to live, and expensive health spells, they would not be poor, then, would they?" asked Lark.

That made Tris look down. She scuffed her foot along the wooden floor.

"I know you are upset," Lark continued in that quiet, disappointed tone that made the girls wish they could hide. "You four have not spent a night apart since you came to us, and the spinning of your magics has made you closer than siblings. But you must not let distress make you cruel. Rosethorn is there because it is the way of the Circle to help all, not just those who can pay. Briar went there because that is the soil in which he grew."

With each word Tris seemed to shrink a little more. Lark never scolded them.

"She didn't mean it," offered Sandry, hoping to make peace.

"Whether she did or not is beside the point. No one asks to live in squalor, Tris. It is just that squalor is all that is left to them by those with money." Lark stood, her shoulders drooping. "When I got the wheezes, what the healers call asthma, I couldn't work as a tumbler anymore. The only place I could afford to live was the Mire."

She walked into her workroom and closed the door. Tris ran upstairs, sniffling. Sandry went into her ground-floor room as Daja walked over to Briar's open door. Little Bear looked up at her, tail fluttering. Daja sat next to him and let the dog put his head in her lap. Outside she could hear the light patter of rain deepen as it fell harder than ever.

Steepling her hands before her face, Daja whispered the prayer her people spoke each night before they went to sleep: "Trader, watch over those of our kindred, in port or at sea. Send them fair winds to speed them home."

Some time after Niko had left, Briar heard the inside door rattle. Someone was pushing things through the lower flap: a large metal box with straps to hold it closed, jars of liquids and salves, a second water kettle in addition to the one that had already been in the room.

Flick had woken from her doze and seemed restless. "What's all that?" she asked as Rosethorn and Briar carried the new supplies to the table.

"Things to help me care for you and to help others unravel what your pox is," said Rosethorn.

Curious, Flick got out of bed and came to sit with

41

them. She propped her chin on her elbows and scratched one of the raised bumps on her cheek.

"Stop that," Rosethorn ordered. "If you feel well enough to walk around, you're well enough to have some juice."

As Rosethorn poured a cupful for their patient, Briar ran his fingers over the metal box. Like the gauze screens on the outer door, it was written over with signs for health and purity, pressed into the metal and worked into the leather straps.

"Sickness is a real thing, as real as air or insects," Rosethorn explained to Flick, taking the box and undoing the straps. "We can't see it without help, but that doesn't mean it isn't there. With the right magics and tools, you can uncover what disease has tainted." Some of this she'd taught Briar over the last year. "That means we take samples not only from those with the disease but also from the ones close to them. We hope to get a look at the early stages of the sickness, before it turns mean. I wish I'd thought to keep a grip on your friend Alleypup. We need him for this."

Rosethorn worked off the box's tight-fitting lid. Inside lay stacks of square white cloth pads. Each was paired with an undyed bag that sported a paper tag on its drawstring. Beside those were flat plates made of glassy black rock and another stack of cloth masks. Briar also noted a tightly stoppered and wax-sealed bottle of liquid ink and a pair of writing brushes.

All of these things were in a tray that fitted inside the box.

"Whatever you see here is spelled to keep every influence out but the samples that go into these bags," Rosethorn told Flick. "Nothing is dyed, the materials are all the most basic. The only thing the mages who work with this stuff should collect is the disease, mixed with the body fluids of the people we get samples from."

The woman lifted out the top tray to show an inner compartment. It held a second, smaller metal box, spelled just as strongly as the one in which it sat. "We send this back to Winding Circle with the samples. It's magicked to keep those who carry it from getting sick." This box she placed on the table. "They'll send us a new one every day."

Rosethorn then took square and bag pairs from the top part of the box, holding them by the edges as she placed five on a black stone plate. Handing the plate to Briar, she returned the top tray and its contents to the large metal box. "Don't touch anything," she warned Flick as the girl looked inside the metal container.

Flick blinked heavy-lidded eyes. "No, Dedicate," she said obediently. "How does all this work?"

"To craft spells that unlock the nature of this disease, a mage needs samples of matter from the sick person. It's drawn from the inside of the mouth, sores or sweat, blood, dung, and urine." Rosethorn sat next to Flick. "For you, the blood part is easy." She pressed a cloth square to Flick's mouth, where a crack in her lower lip bled sluggishly. "Bag," Rosethorn told Briar.

He took the small bag that came with the square by the edges and held it open. When Rosethorn dropped the square in, he pulled the drawstring tight. "Stick out your tongue," Rosethorn ordered Flick.

Briar watched, holding and closing the bags, as Rosethorn pressed a square to Flick's coated tongue and made her blow her nose into another. She helped the street rat into the privy for dung and urine. Once the last sample had been gathered, Rosethorn placed all of Flick's bags on the table and lifted the ink and brushes from the box. "You can do this," she told Briar. "Write the name of the person who gave the sample on the tags, and the date. Be neat." She picked up another stack of bags on a stone tray. "I'll get my samples now."

As she went into the washroom, Briar began to fill out the labels, grinning. All winter, as he struggled to learn to write clearly, Rosethorn had insisted on doing her own labels. That she wanted him to do them now meant his work finally pleased her. Carefully he inscribed *Flick, Fifth Day, Sap Moon, KF*—for after the fall of the Kurchal Empire, the calendar used by all residents of the Pebbled Sea—*1036* on each scrap of parchment. Flick, her head on her arms, watched Briar with sleepy fascination.

"Ain't you never seen a market scribe do this?" Briar wanted to know.

"Everybody expects *them* to write. I never knew anybody myself that could."

Briar grinned. "It ain't easy, but it's fun," he replied, unable to resist a small boast.

Rosethorn watched as he labeled her samples, then gave him more squares, bags, and a tray. "Your turn," she ordered. "Use the thorn to get blood, do your best with your dung and urine. Don't take forever. I want these to reach Winding Circle before dark."

Briar frowned at the tray. "What about them soldiers in the other quarantine?" he wanted to know. "Do we get theirs?"

Rosethorn shook her head. "They've been trained specially for times like this. They do their own. Now hop to it."

When he returned, Rosethorn placed all the samples in the smaller box, then replaced the lid. It clicked into place as she slid it onto the bottom half of the container. When she tested the lid, it refused to come off. The box shone bright silver in Briar's eyes, a sign that the strong protection spells had gone to work.

"How will they get at the samples?" he asked as Rosethorn carried the box to the inside door.

She rapped on it hard. "It's a lock-spell," she replied. "When this is delivered to Winding Circle, those who study the disease have the counter-spell to open it."

45

"Scorching," murmured Flick. "Wish we'd had a lock-spell when the Mudrunners raided our den."

There was a rattling on the other side of the door, and the lower flap opened. Rosethorn put the small box on the floor and gave it a shove. Once it had gone through the opening, the flap closed. The bolt slid into place as the door was locked again.

"Scorching?" asked Rosethorn, lifting one graceful eyebrow. "Mudrunners?"

"Scorching means 'good,' " Briar translated. "Mudrunners is a Mire gang."

"Charming," Rosethorn said drily. "The language *I* speak is so drab by comparison." Pouring a cup of fruit juice, she gave it to Flick.

Flick scowled. "Why do I have to keep drinking this muck?" she demanded.

"You're feverish," Rosethorn told her, more patient than she had ever been with Briar. "You're drying out. Get too dry, and you won't be able to keep fighting the sickness. Look at it this way, it's better than willowbark tea." Coaxing, joking, and being firm by turns, she got the sick girl to finish the juice, then helped her back to bed. Once she had lain down, Rosethorn produced a jar of aloe balm and began to smooth it into Flick's pox-mottled skin.

Briar had seen Rosethorn be gentle as she tied up bean plants, coaxed grapevines to wind more firmly around a trellis, or patched a tree that had lost a limb in a storm. This was the first time he'd seen her use

46

that delicate touch on a human. She could have been the girl's mother, had Flick's mother loved her kid, he thought.

Flick dozed, lulled by silence and Rosethorn's kind touch.

"Niko said you don't like people," Briar remarked softly when Rosethorn came back to the table.

"I don't like nursing them," was her quiet reply.

"But you go to Urda's House and the healers at the City Temple every month," he pointed out. "*Every* month, rain or no. And you always take stuff—"

"I check medicines and replenish them if they are running low," Rosethorn told him. "Especially here, where their goods are the cheapest money can buy, I spell their medicines to the greatest strength magic can give. I don't go near the sick."

"If you're magicking stuff, why didn't you make me stay and watch?"

She smiled crookedly. "Boy, I teach you six and seven days a week at times. Every now and then we both need a rest."

He turned that over in his mind. He *did* like their days in the city, when he was free to go with Flick and her friends, if he wasn't visiting the market with the girls. "You're being nice to Flick," he said at last.

"You needn't adore humanity to feel bad for someone in this fix," she replied. "Street rat or no, she's sick and frightened. There's a difference between people like her and adults who think they know more about your life, and their illness, than you do. If you've nothing better to do than chatter, you can help take inventory of these cupboards. If we get more patients in here, I don't want to run out of anything important."

By the time the clock on top of the Winding Circle tower known as the Hub rang three in the afternoon, Daja had come to work at the big table. Before her lay a spool of thick iron wire, cutters, a thin-tipped punch, and a small hammer and pliers, the tools needed to make chain mail. She was threading a link through its neighbors when she heard a familiar voice in the road that ran past the cottage.

"Don't whine at me, woman! A lack of planning in the Water Temple should *not* be an emergency for *me!*"

The pliers slipped from Daja's fingers. Frostpine yelling? He was usually the most easygoing of men. When she'd left him earlier that day, he had been lazy with good humor over the success of the morning's work.

She ran to the door and threw it open. The rain had stopped. Her teacher, Dedicate Frostpine of the Fire Temple, was striding through the front gate. He looked like a thundercloud about to spit lightning.

A thin, fluttery, pale-skinned woman in the blue habit of the Water Temple followed him. "Your language is intemperate!" she cried.

Frostpine whirled to glare down at her. His brown skin was flushed; his eyes blazed. His wild mane of side-hair and beard gave him the look of a bald lion. His bright red habit, scarred with burns and soot, made him an even more vivid figure. He pointed at the Water dedicate with a finger that trembled with frustration. "'*Intemperate*'?" he repeated. "Gods bless me, you people would make the *moon* intemperate. Last year you ran out of bandages on the eve of a pirate attack, and now, now *this*—"

"How could we have known?" wailed the dedicate. "We have enough for normal diseases. Who would have dreamed a new one could appear and we might need ten times our supply!"

By this time Lark and Sandry had come to see what was going on. Little Bear thrust his big head between Daja's knees for a better view, rocking her. Daja could sense Tris overhead as the redhead watched from an attic window.

"Who would have *dreamed?*" demanded Frostpine. "Who would—! You're *supposed* to dream, of anything, of *every*thing. Now scat!"

The dedicate ran. Frostpine watched her briefly, then stormed into the house. Everyone got out of his way.

"You shouldn't yell at her," Lark said reproachfully.

"Of course I should," Frostpine barked. "Gods bless us all, Lark, but our Water dedicates would try the patience of a *stone!*"

49

"Well, yes," admitted Lark, sitting at the table. "What did they forget this time?"

"The warded boxes, the ones for samples of body fluids from the sick," he said, sinking down on the bench across from her. "They have five."

Lark put a hand to her mouth. "That's not even enough for a disease we know, where all that's needed is to see if it's changed."

"Crane threw a fit—I don't blame him—and sent them to me," Frostpine said bitterly. "If I were Moonstream, I'd scatter the whole lot to the four winds." He looked at Daja. "Bundle up everything you'll need for two or three days," he said with regret. "I can't turn out enough of these boxes on my own. We're going to work till we drop, I'm afraid."

Daja raced upstairs.

"She's leaving too?" asked Sandry. She stood by the household shrine, a bit of forgotten needlework in one hand. Her eyes were huge. "*Three* of us gone?"

"What do you mean, 'three of us'?" Frostpine asked.

Sandry vanished into her room as Lark explained. When Daja came downstairs, Tris in her wake, Frostpine was leaning against Sandry's open door. "So you see, Rosethorn has plenty of experience," he was telling the young noble. "Even if she doesn't know what causes a disease, she's been known to hold them off with sheer force of will." He turned to Daja. "Ready?"

Daja nodded. She gave Little Bear a final scratch around the ears and followed her teacher out of the house.

Sandry ran into her room, to the front window. She waved her handkerchief at Daja and Frostpine as if they were on parade and kept waving until they had gone from view.

"Lark?" she heard Tris say out in the main room. "I'm sorry."

"I know, dear," murmured Lark. "Just remember— your sharp tongue cuts."

Sandry reached into the leather pouch she always wore around her neck and drew out a thread circle. It was thick, undyed wool marked by four lumps, each spaced equally apart, with no way to tell where the thread began or ended. It was the first thing she had ever spun, lumps and all, except that originally it had been just a thread, its two ends separate. It had become a circle when, trapped underground in an earthquake, she had spun the four young people's magics together to make all of them stronger. As far as Sandrilene fa Toren was concerned, that thread *was* the four of them.

As long as *this* is together, *we're* together, she told herself. Even if we aren't in the same house, we're still one.

Briar spent the rest of his first afternoon in quarantine boiling, then hanging up to dry, the cloths used to tend Flick. She was less alert as the afternoon wore on, dozing more or just staring at the ceiling. By sunset Briar almost missed the chores he would have had at Discipline Cottage—they would have been a way to pass time. In Sotat, those of Deadman's District who'd been unfortunate enough to be healthy and quarantined in an epidemic had said it was the most boring part of their lives. As far as Briar could see by that first day's end, they had told the absolute truth. Only the thought of Rosethorn's wrath kept him from finding a way to escape Urda's House.

Before he went to bed, he mind-spoke with all three of the girls. Sandry and Tris were not happy that he and Daja were gone. When Briar complained of boredom, Sandry rapped back, *Good. Pick a birthday.*

Will you stop this birthday folly? he demanded. *There's other stuff on my mind just now!*

You said you were bored, Daja said. *Either you're bored and need something to think about, or you're too busy to be bored.*

Vexed with them, he went to sleep and dreamed of the last plague to hit Hajra. It was cholera, "the dung disease," as they called it. People danced wildly in the street. In the dream he didn't want to dance, but was about to join in anyway, when a bright, steady light shone on his face, waking him.

Rosethorn was seated at Flick's bed, next to his: she had placed her light-stone on the shelf that ran along the wall behind the cots. When Briar sat up, she said quietly, "Get all the sleep you can. You'll need it."

Instead Briar swung his legs out from under the blanket. "What's the gab?" he asked, keeping his voice low.

"I wish you would go back to talking like a real person." Rosethorn blotted Flick's face with a wet cloth.

"He *is* talking like a real person," croaked Flick. "Nobody in the Mire talks like you."

"Briar, go to bed," insisted Rosethorn. "We'll have plenty to do in the morning. Have some more willow-bark tea, Flick."

Briar lay down again, wrapping himself in his blanket. We don't know this pox is a killer, he told himself firmly. Plenty get smallpox or measles and live. Maybe this pox is just a weak measle.

Even if it is a killer, Flick will make it. Rosethorn can save anybody.

Dawn was a bare gleam in the sky when Tris
stumped downstairs. Lark was still abed, her door
closed. Sandry was coming in from the well with a
full bucket, her sleep-tousled brown hair at all angles.
Little Bear, sprawled across the threshold to Briar's
room, lifted his head and whined at Tris.

"Just how I feel," replied Tris, her voice low. "Do
you want to go out?"

The dog got to his feet and went to the front door,
sniffing it as Tris crossed the big room. To her surprise, Little Bear started to growl.

"*Now* what?" she demanded, flinging the door

wide. A tall, lanky man in a black-bordered yellow habit stumbled over the sill: it seemed he had been leaning on the door. Tris and Little Bear jumped out of the way as the dedicate went sprawling. The dog barked hysterically, the fur along his shoulders standing upright. Sandry looked up drowsily, shook her head, and continued the exacting work of pouring water from bucket to kettle.

"I *hate* dogs." The newcomer rolled onto his back and half sat, bracing himself on his elbows.

"What in Mila's name—?" demanded Lark, coming out in her nightgown. She looked at the man and sighed, combing her fingers through her short curls. "Hello, Crane," she said wryly. "Just in time for breakfast." She returned to her room, closing the door.

The first dedicate and chief mage of the Air Temple arched dark, thin brows at Tris. "Will you control the animal?" he asked, his voice wintry. "I should hate to rise and instigate a bout of fierceness."

Tris sighed and gripped Little Bear's collar. "Down," she said firmly.

Little Bear sat. He continued to growl deep in his throat as Dedicate Crane pulled his long arms and legs together and got to his feet. He was the kind of man who never just stood, but draped himself on air. His expressive hands always dangled from the wrists, as if they were too elegant to disappear into his pockets. Crane had a long face and a long nose, a small, pursed mouth, and weary brown eyes. Even his black hair, cut earlobe-length and brushed back, drooped.

Tris rubbed her nose, eyeing the man suspiciously. Briar's *shakkan* had belonged to Crane originally—the boy had stolen it from Crane's greenhouse. It meant the first meeting between Crane and the four had been unpleasant. Later they had discovered that Rosethorn and Crane were rivals in plant magic. "What were you doing?" asked the redhead. "Leaning on the door?"

Up went the eyebrows; Crane's eyes ran over her chubby form. "One does expect a modicum of manners in the young," he remarked drily.

"Good for one," retorted Tris. "If you wanted manners, you should have come after I had my tea."

"I'm brewing as fast as I can," Sandry informed her with a yawn, placing the kettle on the fire. "Why don't you take Little Bear out?"

Tris obeyed while Sandry fetched cream and honey and placed them on the table. Crane had seated himself there without a word. Unaware of Sandry's gaze, he had lowered his face into his hands and was rubbing his eyes. The young noble suddenly wondered when he had slept that night, or even if he had.

The brows, and bloodshot eyes, rose over the screen of fingers. "You are staring," he said, voice muffled by his hands.

Sandry made a face and turned to get the cups. Something twinged near her heart as she gathered Lark's, Tris's, and her own cup and passed over those that belonged to the missing three. Last she grabbed one of the spares and placed them all on the table, then entered Rosethorn's workroom. In a corner near the kitchen were the jars with their teas, each mixed by Rosethorn to her exacting taste. Using a dish, Sandry ladled out the morning blend, a sunny tea heavy with rosehips and bits of lemon peel. She resealed that jar and hesitated, her eyes going to the jar labeled *Endurance*. Finally she removed a spoonful, dusting it over the mound of morning blend.

Who can't use a little endurance in times like these? she asked as she resealed that jar. No one, that's who. Taking the dish to the hearth, she poured the contents into the teapot strainer. Once the kettle boiled, she added water to the pot and carried it over to the table.

Tris had returned and was seated across from Crane, slicing a loaf of fruit bread. Sandry wanted to sigh. Tris's blue wool gown was rumpled; her wiry copper hair strained at the scarf she used to tie it away from her face. Sandry reached out and brushed her fingertips against Tris's skirt. A touch of light skipped through the weave as the wrinkles dropped out, leaving the cloth as neat as if it had been pressed.

"I would have thought you'd be in your workroom, Crane, not paying calls," Lark said, emerging from her bedroom. She had combed her glossy curls and donned a green habit. The shadows under her eyes were untouched. "Who's helping you?"

"Some novices, a few Water Temple initiates." Crane flapped his long fingers as if shooing the Water dedicates out of his presence. "This is not a social visit."

"You need to talk to Rosethorn?" inquired Lark as she sat at the table. "We could arrange it through Sandry or Tris and Briar—"

Crane shook his head. "This is—I mean, I—I would like to request—"

Lark sighed and picked up a piece of bread. "Crane, it's too early for you to dance like a kitten. You know I'll help you if I can."

Sandry passed a slice of bread to Crane, who began to pick it apart. "It's the masks, and the gloves," he said at last, without looking up.

"Don't tell me Water Temple's short on those too," Lark said crossly. "I swear, I'll go to Moonstream herself—" She stopped abruptly; Crane was shaking his head.

"They have plenty, all with protective signs woven into them, as is standard," he replied. "To deal with normal contagion they are perfect. My work is somewhat different. I must refine the disease into its essence, then experiment until we can develop a method of magical diagnosis. Manipulating pox samples, finding those substances to which it reacts—the risks are great that my staff and I will be exposed before we are able to fight the disease. Water Temple healers at least have enough raw power to burn it from their own bodies if they must, but we are not all

58

healers. I want my people to be safe. As things stand, we feel as if we dance on a fire in paper shoes."

Lark reached across the table, holding a hand out to him. After a moment's hesitation, Crane slid his elegant fingers into her palm. "You'd like us to add a layer to your protections," she said, her dark eyes grave.

Tris, listening hard, poured the tea into cups. Sandry kept very still, though her blue eyes were wide with interest.

Crane nodded, a blush creeping under his pallid skin. "I know it is difficult," he said apologetically. "I realize that the general supply of masks and gloves may run low and you will be called on to help supply all of our healers."

"Actually, you've given me the solution to a problem," Lark told him with a smile, giving his hand a pat before she released it. She accepted her teacup from Sandry as Tris gave the guest's cup to Crane. "I wanted to teach Sandry how spells are laid in cloth after it's woven." To Sandry she explained, "We make up a spelled oil and work it into the fiber. The most powerful kind, the oil we shall need for Crane, must be made up fresh every few days. That means the pace of our work is steady. I won't tell you to do this, but I hope you'll want to help."

"As if I'd say no!" Sandry replied, eager to have something to do.

"Thank you," Crane said with feeling. He drank his

tea in tiny sips, to keep from burning his mouth. Sandry noticed that as he drank, his color improved and he sat a little straighter. She smiled to herself and added cream to her own tea.

"Have you had word from"—they all knew Crane was about to say "Rosethorn," but at the last moment he changed it to—"the city?"

"Flick got worse," both girls said at once, and made faces at each other. Briar had once said they sounded like a Ragat chorus when they spoke the same words.

"She is the child found"—Crane's long nose wrinkled; it seemed he was too elegant to use the word "sewer"—"underground?"

"In the sewer," replied Tris wickedly.

Crane began to eat the fruit bread he had shredded. "Messenger birds arrived from the city just before I came here," he commented between bites. "Two derelicts who sleep in Mummer's Close have been found with the disease and taken to Urda's House. In addition, a body covered with blue spots was found last night in an empty lot on Spice Walk. The ailment is definitely contagious, and the mage who examined the body says that it surely caused the man's death."

"Yanna Pain-Taker defend us," said Lark, calling on the goddess of medicine and healers. All of them made the gods-circle on their chests.

Shortly after dawn on Briar's second day of quarantine, a pair of homeless men were brought into the room by masked soldiers of the Duke's Guard. Once the sick men had been washed, dressed in the night-shirts, and put to bed—they were both too feverish to object to the soldiers' handling—the guards joined their fellows in the room next door.

With the addition of the newcomers, Briar soon found that quarantine for anyone involved in healing meant work. Now there were three patients to be cared for in what seemed to be an endless round of washing, balm rubs, chamber pots, and cups of every liquid under the sun. The sharp scent of willowbark tea felt burned into his nostrils. The older of the two men, Yuvosh, was hardly any trouble and did what-ever he was told. His friend, Orji, was not so coopera-tive. He was too hot, too cold, headachy or hungry for real food, not broth or juice. His skin itched; his bones ached; he couldn't sleep for so much as five minutes at a time. He was convinced that every new thing they made him drink was poison. Given the taste of some of the brews Rosethorn created, Briar couldn't exactly blame him.

Flick weakened. What frightened Briar the most was that each time he helped her to sit up for more tea or juice, she felt thinner. The fever that came with the pox was eating the little fat she had. Yuvosh also worried him, but in a less personal way; he was too weak and too obedient. A respectable street rat, even a grown one, should put up more of a fuss, or so it seemed to Briar.

Then there was Rosethorn. Briar worked on her as hard as he did their patients, trying to get her to eat and sleep so that she would stay well. At least she was extra-careful to protect Briar and herself from contagion. She continued to insist they wear masks and gloves unless they ate or cleaned themselves. Tableware and the cloths they used to tend their sick were washed, then immersed in boiling water. She and Briar scrubbed all over once a day, in very hot water, using soaps made to strip the skin of infection. The smell of the soap lingered around them both like an invisible cloud.

Rosethorn would dictate notes or lists of supplies to Briar as she worked on their patients or on the medicines she made from oils and herbs. The supplies of those items passed to them through the big flap on the inner door were never right. When she argued with the people who brought them, they summoned the man who ran Urda's House, Jokubas Atwater. Talking through the speaking-window, Atwater told Rosethorn impatiently that the house was not made of money and she would have to make do, as they did.

The notes Briar wrote for Rosethorn went to Winding Circle, sealed in the metal boxes of samples that were taken every day from all five of them. Notes and samples alike were needed by the healers if they were to see how the disease worked, and Rosethorn's notes were thorough. Her experience of other epidemics meant she knew what to look for in this one. She taught some of her knowledge to Briar, to explain things and as a break from the dull chores of the sickroom.

They had been in quarantine for three days when guards sheathed from head to toe in oilcloth carried in five more patients, all covered with blue spots. Two were younger than Flick; two were old; and the fifth man, who looked to be Orji's age, coughed deep in his chest. With them came a dedicate in the blue Water Temple habit, a plump, wide-hipped woman with dark brown hair and eyes, and skin the color of newly minted bronze. She carried a large basket of supplies on her back.

"Henna," Rosethorn greeted the new arrival. "It's about time."

"I would have come sooner, but they locked me in with that lunatic Crane, until he decided he couldn't stand me. I don't know how you work with him," replied Dedicate Henna, unslinging the basket and its supporting frame. "I decided quarantine is better."

Rosethorn laughed for the first time in days. "You know, I was wondering what I missed about times like this," she commented, throwing back the sailcloth cover on Henna's basket. "It was Crane, hovering and telling me I wouldn't get anywhere with whatever I was doing. You're right—quarantine is preferable."

All three of them—Henna, Rosethorn, and Briar—settled the new patients in, cleaning them up and sending their old clothes down the washroom chute that led straight to a furnace. While they brewed fresh willowbark tea from Henna's supplies, they also took samples from the new patients, sending them out with their own samples for the day. Tea came next; everyone got some. The old people were nearly too weak to sip, which Briar could tell worried the women. Next came balm rubs to soothe their patients' itchy skins.

At last everyone had been tended. Briar and Rosethorn sat at the table as Henna poured cups of a more ordinary rosehip orange tea for them. "I don't know about you, but *I* have a headache," the Water dedicate informed Rosethorn. "You must be tired."

Rosethorn smiled crookedly and drank her tea down.

Briar looked at Henna beseechingly. To say anything in front of Rosethorn was to invite a flailing with the rough edge of her tongue. He could only pray that Henna would see the message in his eyes.

She did. "I'll take over for now," she told Rosethorn briskly. "I want you to drink this broth Dedicate Gorse sent with me, then go to bed. I'll wake you at dusk." Henna rested a hand on Rosethorn's shoulder. "Shame on you for not taking better care of yourself! You're worn to the bone, and your boy here isn't much better off. Same orders for you, my lad," she told Briar sternly. "Broth and bed."

"There's yarrow balm in the yellow jar," Rosethorn

said with a yawn. "We made it up fresh yesterday. Aloe balm in the green one, and—"

"I *know* how you mark your medicines," Henna said tartly. "Broth, bed! Now!"

Rosethorn leaned closer, and kept her voice low. "Why is there only one of you?"

Henna rested a hand on Rosethorn's shoulder. "Because we knew you and Briar here were fine and able to care for this lot, if you had someone else good to help. The others are needed elsewhere. The Duke's Guard started a house-to-house search of the Mire today, and they keep finding new cases. Two of the other three rooms on this floor are starting to fill up. They're calling it the blue pox, you know. The spots show up blue on all but the darkest skins."

Briar saw Rosethorn's fingers tighten on Henna's shoulder, making the cloth dimple. "How *many* new cases?" she whispered. "How many dead?"

"Thirteen dead we know of," was Henna's soft reply. "Only sixty-five sick when I came in. I suspect more are hiding or telling themselves it's just a rash, so there's no way to judge how many are truly ill. I'm guessing from the counts I've seen that probably there are at least a hundred more cases today. If we're lucky."

Rosethorn chewed on her lower lip, thinking. "Where are they finding the sick?"

"North Mire," replied Henna promptly. "From the buildings near the city wall."

Rosethorn sighed. "Yanna willing, this is the worst of it."

"If it doesn't break out of the Mire, we'll avoid a deal of heartache. The guards have orders to stop any Mire dwellers from entering the city." Henna looked at Briar. "Now, my lad, get rid of that long face and dish up the broth for you two." She pointed to a large, wax-sealed crock.

He did as he was told. Sipping his—no matter how hard he worked, he remembered to eat—he watched as Rosethorn drank her broth. When she finished, he followed her to her cot. "Thank the gods for Honored Moonstream," Rosethorn commented softly as she slid under her blanket. "She's no coin-pincher, unlike the people who run this place. With Henna in here we'll get the supplies we need from Winding Circle."

What we needed most was help, Briar thought, watching as Rosethorn went right to sleep. And we got it.

He went to bed. Lying down was one thing, he found; sleeping was something else. Had he given Flick willowbark tea that morning? In the last three days Rosethorn had taught him a slavish love for willowbark. It was the only thing that lowered the fever, which fretted her more than the spots and the sores that developed when the spots cracked open. The tea also soothed her other worry, that Flick was drying out, though Rosethorn used a different word: dehydration.

66

Perhaps he should check the slate at the foot of Flick's cot. He would have marked it if he'd given his friend willowbark tea that morning.

Henna sat on Orji's cot, holding the sick man's wrists. Running from her fingers was a tracery of silver—magic. Briar closed his eyes for a moment, then looked again. The tracery was clearer, threading from dedicate to man like rootlets. Fascinated, Briar walked over to watch.

The magic streamed along Orji's arms and into his body, as if Henna ran it through his veins. For a long, long moment Henna's power bathed Orji from top to toe. At last it retreated, trickling out of his body the way it had come in. Once Henna got her magic back, she released the dozing man and folded her hands in her lap, head bowed.

Briar was about to creep away when she spoke. "*You* are supposed to be sleeping." Her voice had the trained quiet of someone who spends her time with the sick: Briar heard clearly, but neither Orji nor Flick in the next bed stirred.

"I couldn't. What magic was that, what you did?"

Henna swiveled to look up at him. "You know I was doing magic?"

"It's a thing I picked up from Tris," he replied. Not long after Sandry had spun their magics together, Niko had written a spell on Tris's spectacles, helping her to see magic as he did. The skill then spread to Daja, Sandry, and Briar through their bond with Tris,

67

just as Tris learned a little of their magics. "I see power when it's moving or working," Briar explained to Henna, "but I don't know what it's doing."

Henna moved over to Flick's cot, sat, and took Flick's hands. The street girl stirred, opening heavy-lidded eyes. "I just want to see how you are," Henna reassured her.

Flick glanced up at Briar, who nodded. "I'm fine," she whispered, licking dry lips.

Briar fetched a cup of water and held Flick up so she could drink. When she turned her face away, he lowered her to the pillow again. As Flick's eyes closed, Henna closed her own.

"It's a thing healers learn to do," she murmured. Around her hands sprouted a web of light-strands that sank into Flick's dark-spotted arms and raced through her body. "Before we start work, we must first know what is wrong. It may be that the treatment we put to a fever will hurt the patient's diseased kidneys, or the foxglove we give to strengthen a heartbeat may cause a weakened heart to fail."

"Then you can see what the blue pox is," Briar said eagerly.

Henna shook her head. "If it were a disease I had fought before, perhaps I could sense it, but only then. This isn't even *related* to the diseases I know. But I can see the flow of her blood, the strength of her heart and kidneys and bowels. I can feel her muscles, brain, and bones. I can see weak blood, if she has it, or

68

fluid in the lungs. Bad eating habits, certainly." Henna wrinkled her nose. "And worms, and flukes."

Flick's mouth dropped open. Her breath rattled in her dry mouth and nose. She was asleep.

"Worms and flukes?" asked Briar, not sure he'd heard right.

"Parasites, in her body. They live on her. I would imagine, before Rosethorn cleaned her up, she had lice and fleas as well."

Briar was about to ask, "Don't everybody?" when he remembered that he had not since his arrival at Winding Circle. Who am I? he wondered for a moment, shocked. Who am I really? It's like I shucked being Roach the street rat like worn-out clothes—but Roach is who I was for years. I can't just strip away *years*, can I?

"Where is this girl from?" Henna was asking. "Where did she live?"

Briar frowned at her. "The sewer," he said irritably. He didn't like the disapproval in Henna's face and voice. Where else could Flick live and be safe? he wanted to ask, but did not. Instead he thought, Henna acts like I'm one of her kind, one of the citizens. And I'm not. I can't be.

Henna shook her head and reclaimed her magic. Gently she drew the blanket over Flick's thin arms. "She will have a battle of it, I'm afraid."

"We'll pull her through," Briar said confidently. "I've heard them at the Circle—they say you're one of

69

the best. I'll do whatever you say. I was thinking maybe Flick could do with more willowbark tea."

"I'll take care of that," said Henna, regarding him with an odd expression in her eyes. "You should rest."

"I don't mind—"

"All our patients are asleep now, so I don't mind either. Bed."

Briar turned to go. He was halfway across the floor when her soft yet clear voice reached his ears. "Sometimes there's nothing you can do, boy—Briar. Sometimes they don't have enough to fight with."

He looked back at her. "Flick'll fight. You'll see." He fell on his bed and rolled the blanket around him. *Maybe for a birthday I should pick the day when Roach of Deadman's District kicked the bucket and left this kid Briar in his place,* he thought tiredly. *Except I don't even know when that was. It all happened in bits and pieces, like.*

Maybe the girls know when it was.

Sleep, like the change from Roach to Briar, came slowly. Somewhere, between thought and dreams, he flowed along the invisible ties that stretched between him and the girls. It turned his dreams to small chunks of their lives.

He was Daja, bent over a sheet of iron beaten leather-thin as Kirel, Frostpine's other apprentice, bludgeoned away on a nearby anvil. Heat pressed Daja/Briar from the right, drawing her skin tight on that side while a cold, damp blast made her left side pebble with goosebumps. The grip of a sharp-edged tool she thought of as a "graver" nestled firmly in her right hand.

Slowly she thrust the sharp point of the graver along the iron, shaping the curves that would form the symbol for protection. Her magic flowed in the graver's wake. It called the power to shield and to hold out of the metal. She followed a magical trail, Briar realized: there was a design already drawn on the metal in rose geranium oil and Frostpine's magic. It combined with Daja's as she cut four half circles into the metal, each combining with the others to shape four petals. Last of all she cut a full circle that passed through the other curves. As she completed it, running into the point where she had begun, the magic faded, power seeping into iron to fill every inch. At last it was just a dimly glowing set of curves in her eyes.

A hand—large, warm, callused—came down on her shoulder. There was no telling how long Frostpine had been there, watching. She looked up into his proud eyes. "Very good," he said. "The best yet. One more, and I think we are finished for the day."

Briar lost Daja, but magic tugged him still. He found himself in Sandry's mind as she labored with mortar and pestle in Lark's workroom.

Charcoal to filter out the bad, rose geranium for protection, she was thinking—Briar noticed that both Lark and Frostpine liked to use rose geranium. Sandry worked her pestle around the mortar's bowl in a steady rhythm, thrusting her magic into her ingredients. Granules of frankincense flattened under her rocking pressure, mixing with the liquid in crushed flower petals and rosemary leaves. Protection and purification, Sandry thought; no shadow can enter. She filled the bowl to the brim with her power. Carnation and frankincense oils strengthened and purified what would be a thin paste rather than an oil. In a corner of her mind the noble drew and redrew a protective circle in white fire around those she loved. Peering at those within her circle, Briar recognized himself, Rosethorn, the girls, Lark, Frostpine, Niko, Little Bear, the duke—and Dedicate Crane?

The surprise of seeing Crane made him wake on his cot at Urda's House. He blinked at the ceiling. Why in Trickster Lakik's name did Sandry care what happened to Crane?

Sitting up, Briar looked around. Henna sat next to one of the new kids' beds. A silver shimmer marked the flow of magic through her fingers into her patient. It chased a blue tint out of the boy's unpocked skin.

Briar went over for a closer look. "What's the matter with him?" he whispered.

"He had a seizure—a convulsion—while you were asleep," she replied. "It happens when a fever runs too long unchecked. He's blue all over because he didn't get enough air during the spasms, so I'm trying to change that."

Briar watched the flow of her magic, intent. Henna's power followed the veins between the child's chest and his head. "How does magic in his blood fix his air?"

"Haven't you learned *any* physiology—how the body works?" asked Henna, startled.

Briar scowled at the hint that Rosethorn wasn't teaching him properly. "I do plants," he said, "not people."

Henna shook her head. "I would have thought— never mind," she added as Briar glared at her. "Veins— blood—carry air from the lungs to the brain. Without air, even for a short time, parts of the brain start to die. It can mean a change as tiny as forgetting how to tie a knot, or it can lead to idiocy, even death. Some who survive the blue pox will live damaged, even crippled."

The sick boy opened his eyes, staring at Henna. "I'll be there, Mama," he whispered. "Don't let the camels eat me." He went back to sleep.

"He's got a chance to survive." Henna released him and got to her feet. Sighing, she turned her head and neck in a circle, trying to relax stiff muscles. "His family came on hard times just recently, so he's still healthy at bottom. If we keep his brain whole, he may do all right."

They had put the man with the cough in a distant corner, away from the old people and the children. Now he sat up, hacking loudly.

"What about him?" asked Briar.

Henna shook her head. "He's in the last stages of consumption—lung-rot. Catching the blue pox just means he'll die sooner rather than later."

"But you could heal him," protested Briar in a whisper, following her to the cupboards as she hunted for something. "I've seen you people do healings. Why aren't you at it now?"

Henna pulled a basin from the cupboard. "I have the power to heal four of the people in this room completely," she said, her voice tight. "Old people and children and those already ill, like that man, are the hardest to bring back—I'd have to go to Death's kingdom to get them. That will drain me for a month or more—that means I'd be useless, bedridden, too weak even to care for the sick without my magic. If healers use themselves up to save a handful, what happens to the sick brought in tomorrow, and the next day, and the day after?" She searched through the medicines on the table, taking a brown glass bottle. "Get a cup."

Briar obeyed.

As Henna poured liquid from the bottle into the cup, she continued, "A touch of my power given to one person at a time might help fifty to win free of the disease, and leave me with enough magic to fight the blue pox in my own body. I may have to let some die, if they're too far gone, and keep my power to save others."

74

"I'm sorry," Briar whispered as she thrust the stopper into the bottle.

"So am I," replied Henna. "It's the single worst thing about being a healer-mage." She took the cup and basin to the coughing man.

One of the old people sat up. "Get that oar in the water, ye sluggard," she cried. "We're bringin' home a full boat if we fish till midnight!" She gasped and choked.

Rosethorn was beside her before Briar knew his teacher was awake, thrusting a cloth between the old woman's teeth. The woman bucked hard, convulsing, and threw Rosethorn off the bed. Briar ran to help.

There was no quiet moment after that. Both the old woman and the boy had seizures all afternoon. When they were quiet, Henna, Rosethorn, and Briar cleaned everyone up and tried to get liquids into them. The man with consumption coughed long and often, fighting to breathe. By sunset he was spitting blood into the basin Henna had brought to him.

Flick dozed lightly at times or blinked at the ceiling. She was still too weak to sit. Briar helped the girl up, desperately trying to get her to drink more.

The thin gray daylight was fading when Briar heard the clank of metal. He dropped the bowl he was scrubbing and looked for the source. Was it the outside door again?

There was the sound of a bolt being drawn: *clack*.

The inner door, the one that opened into Urda's House, swung open.

Rosethorn and Henna got to their feet. Jokubas Atwater, the mean old man who had told Rosethorn that Urda's House was not made of money, stood in the open door. "This entire building is now a pesthouse," he said acidly, eyes bitter. "The sick must keep to their own floors, but healers"—he looked around until he found Briar—"and apprentices, you may move freely about the house."

"We could use another pair of hands," remarked Henna.

"You'll get them," Jokubas said crisply. "My daughter is coming up here now, with ten more sick."

The news that Briar and Rosethorn had been joined by Dedicate Henna was greeted with relief at Discipline Cottage. Everyone went to bed early that night, tired by worry and their own labors. Tris woke sometime after midnight to the sound of rain tapping the thatch overhead. She put on her spectacles, a wool gown, and a shawl, sending her power out. The familiar sense of hot metal in the room across from hers was missing—she frowned, then remembered that Daja was at Frostpine's, working and sleeping at his forge. With a sigh Tris let her magic seep through the boards and plaster between her and the ground floor. Lark slept heavily, the warmth of her magic lower than Tris had ever felt it. Sandry was in the same shape. They had worked hard, putting their strength into the masks and gloves for Crane and his staff.

Tris found Little Bear's life force, that of a dozing animal with unhappy dreams. He had to be sleeping in Briar's room again: her sense of him was nearly overpowered by the magic that radiated from Briar's *shakkan*. Over its one-hundred-forty-six-year existence, the miniature tree had been used to store and build upon the magic of its earlier owners; its green strength pressed on her own power. There was a curiously similar feel to the *shakkan* and to Little Bear, a kind of sadness. They missed Briar.

"We all do," she muttered crossly, stuffing her feet into thin leather slippers. "Can't you keep it to yourselves?"

With the stealth of months of practice she left the house, though she wondered why she bothered to be quiet. From the feel of Sandry and Lark, Tris thought that she might bang kettle lids in their ears and they wouldn't twitch.

Through the back gate she passed, then between the fence and the vineyard. Over the winter she had worn a path in the grass, one that led across a band of open ground. It went straight to the closest stair on the inside of Winding Circle's thick wall. The rain fell steadily as she climbed, hoisting her skirts to keep from tripping, panting with effort. At least these days no one who saw her puffing was silly enough to yell at her to lose weight. Before she had learned to control her power—and the way it produced hail or lightning when she was vexed—some had teased her, with interesting results.

Learning to control her magic had meant she had to give up rewarding those people who gave cruel advice. She hadn't liked that, even when Niko pointed out that those she frightened became enemies. Niko is a spoilsport, thought Tris, trying to catch her breath as she stepped onto the top of the wall.

Most nights when she came up here, she walked south to get a view of the harbor islands and the Pebbled Sea beyond. There was no glimpse of the sea tonight; the rain cloaked it. Below and to her right lay the joining of the roads that wrapped around Winding Circle and the granite ridge between the temple and the Mire. The slum and even walled Summersea were gone from view; no light cut through the rain, not even that of the harbor beacons.

"One day—" a quiet voice began.

Tris gasped and jumped. Niko's approach had taken her by surprise. He steadied the girl with a hand on her shoulder. She could barely see his craggy face under the wide-brimmed hat he'd worn to keep off the wet.

"I didn't mean to frighten you," he said.

"Well, you did," muttered Tris. "What were you going to say?"

"Only that if you ever get a home of your own, you ought to consider a nice tower, preferably on a cliff. You seem to prefer lookout spots."

"I'm a weather mage, aren't I?" she asked. "Of course I like heights."

"Tell me, weather mage, how long you do expect this storm to last?"

Tris sent her power rolling into the clouds. "A day, maybe two," she replied, testing the feel of water, heat, and cold in the air. "Hard rain toward dawn, mistylike until ten in the morning, light rain after."

"Can you make it end? Usher the storm away from here?"

Tris stared at him. "You just asked me to meddle with the weather."

"Yes." He evaded her eyes, staring out at the dark landscape.

"But you threatened dire things if I used my power like that. I'm not allowed to muck with nature."

"This is different."

"How do you know *your* telling me to do it won't turn out as badly as if I did it on my own?" she demanded.

"I don't," was the flat reply. "I feel it's important enough to try, though, or I never would have brought it up."

80

That made her nervous. "Please explain," she said, unusually meek.

Niko sighed. "It seems this disease isn't carried in the air, which is the only good news we've had all week. That leaves human contact, insects or animals, or water. If animals were carriers, we would have noticed sick ones. There are no flies or mosquitoes at this time of year, though we can't rule out fleas and lice. I believe this thing spreads too quickly to be simply a matter of human contact, though Crane won't rule that out. The only thing we can try to change—"

"Is water," said Tris.

"The water in the sewers rises by the hour," said Niko. "It may already be leaking into the city's wells. It certainly will do so if the water continues to rise. If we can move this rain along, our outlook would be improved."

Tris removed her shoes, spectacles, and shawl, handing them to Niko. She climbed into one of the flat-bottomed notches in the top of the wall and turned away from the wind. The storm was at her back, coming from the southeast, bound for the northern mountains. She spread herself in it and let its motion thrust her to its leading edge. The hills around Summersea rolled under her. Rivers, streams, towns, she felt them all as she flowed overhead, bound for the great mountains beyond.

An opposing wind in her face brought her to a halt. Here was a pressure to counter the storm she

81

rode, a whirling mass of air entrenched nearly thirty miles to the north. It would go nowhere; if she insisted, she would regret it. She had met such things before and wouldn't have cared if she'd had no storm at her back to move along.

She jumped onto the edge of the unmoving northern system. Following its edge west as she sought a gap where she could put her storm, she found none. At last she gave up. Returning to the storm over Winding Circle, she used its power to send her shooting high above the clouds into open air. Safe from her storm's pull, she turned west again, still looking for a space to move it to. There was nothing she would not have to fight other weather to clear.

Cat dirt, thought Tris, using a favorite expression of Sandry's.

Curious, she sank until she was caught up in her storm's counterclockwise spin. She let it drag her south and east, saving her own strength for the return trip. At the storm's southernmost point she yanked free. A fresh storm caught her almost instantly. She let it pull her even farther south and jumped free— straight into a third storm.

When at last she opened her body's eyes, she found that the sky showed barely pink through a small break in the eastern clouds. A fine drizzle fell on Winding Circle.

Her body had gone stiff in her absence. She

lurched and saw there was but an inch between her feet and the edge of the wall. She'd forgotten she stood in a notch, with nothing to keep her from walking into thin air.

A wiry arm circled her waist and yanked her back. Tris and Niko both tumbled to the walkway in an undignified pile.

When she rolled off him, Niko sat up, gasping for air. "Don't *ever* do that by yourself!" he scolded when he caught his breath. "You might have been killed!"

"I noticed," replied Tris, shuddering.

Niko fumbled at his belt, producing a flask. He opened it and put it to her lips. Tris drank obediently, trying not to let the sweet tea leak between her chattering teeth. It was a mixture she didn't recognize, flavored with dates, citron, and plums.

"That isn't one of Rosethorn's," she gasped when she was done. She didn't need to see the magic that infused the tea; she felt it in her veins. Her head cleared, and her chilled body warmed quickly.

"Moonstream fixed it," replied Niko, returning the flask to his belt. "I assume you were gone so long for a reason—have you good news for me?"

Tris lurched to her feet, wringing her very wet skirts. Niko remained on the walkway, staring up at her, eyes bright under his broad-brimmed hat.

Taking a deep breath, Tris said, "I can move this storm, but it won't mean anything. There are storms behind it for hundreds of miles. They're dumping rain over the whole east half of the Pebbled Sea. Whatever I send off will be replaced in a day, even less."

Niko's heavy brows snapped together in a frown. "Why now, O Gods?" he demanded. "Why give us all this rain now? We don't need—"

"Hoy!" someone yelled from below, inside Winding Circle. "I was told Niklaren Goldeye is up there!"

"How could anyone know that?" asked Tris as Niko got up.

"While you were—busy," he said drily, "I had several chats with the guards. They must have told him." He leaned over the edge of the walkway. "One moment," he called. Walking briskly to the stair, Tris behind him, he descended.

Their summoner looked happy to wait: he was bracing himself on spread knees as he fought to catch his breath. Tris was interested to see he wore the uniform not of the Duke's Guard—which looked after the Mire and everything else outside Summersea's wall—but of the Provost's Guard, which patrolled inside it.

"They said you was to know right off," the man wheezed when they reached him. "Someone told our cap'n, and she ordered us to search the house, and we found three of 'em. And then she ordered us, do the flanking houses, and we got three more in one and five in t'other. Cap'n's turning out all Cobbler's Lane now. You're wanted in town."

84

Niko held up a hand, his expression bleak. "Three, three, and five what?" he asked, his light voice slightly husky.

The guard took a deep breath, and straightened. "It's the blue pox, Master Goldeye," he said, his eyes haunted. "Inside the city wall."

After a long night in which more time was spent caring for the sick than sleeping, Briar, Rosethorn, Henna, and the new healer were treated to gruel, tea, and the prospect of a busy day. No sooner had they finished breakfast than the women were called to a meeting of all the healers in Urda's House. "Stay put," Rosethorn murmured to Briar. "There will be a lot of quarreling before anything useful is discussed. Your time is better spent here."

Briar stayed and watched as those not at the meeting—House workers and members of the Duke's Guard, all gloved and masked—carried in more patients. By noon every bed was filled. Workers then laid pallets in the broad center aisle. Once those were made up, ten more sick were brought in. A screen was put around the coughing man. He had survived the night, but his breath now bubbled horribly in his throat.

Intimidated by the new adults, not liking the fact that they tended patients without gentleness, Briar stayed beside Flick's bed. He left only to fetch water, visit the privy, or fill cups from the big pot of broth and the bigger one of willowbark tea set up on the table.

Outside the night's storm continued: its winds moaned through the cracks in the walls. As workers brought fresh lamps to relieve the gloom, Briar made a happy discovery. The spots on Flick were shrinking and fading. When Rosethorn came back, he dragged her to Flick's bed. "The pocks are going!" he said gleefully. "She'll make it!"

Rosethorn took Flick's pulse, then tried the heat on the girl's forehead and chest. "Still feverish, though not as much," she remarked. "We'll just have to see." She looked up at Briar, who scowled at her calm way of receiving the best news he'd had in a while. "She *may* be on the mend. That fever is more dangerous than the spots—I don't like how it resists the willowbark. In any event, you have to leave her for a while. We have work to do."

"Who'll look after her?" demanded Briar.

"The people who work up here, for now," said Rosethorn.

"But they aren't careful. They just poke the sick ones and go."

Rosethorn frowned. Briar huddled into his clothes, expecting to get the rough side of her tongue. She looked to be in that kind of mood.

Instead she took a breath and resettled the strings that held her mask around her ears, getting her temper in hand. "They'll look after your friend as well as anyone. There is work for plant mages, and it must be done now."

Briar put his cups down with a sigh and followed her out. They passed three other large rooms like theirs on the way to the inner staircase. Those wards were filled too. More than half of the people who worked in them wore the blue habits of the Water Temple, a sight that comforted Briar. Though the new healer in their room, Atwater's daughter, seemed all right, he had never met any of the others who worked in Urda's House. What he did know, from Rosethorn's tales of arguments with them over the winter, did not leave him with much confidence in the locals.

"Why serve here, if they don't like poor people?" he asked Rosethorn as they descended the stairs.

She smiled crookedly. "Some care. Some do it because it's fashionable these days to take an interest in the Mire," she explained. "Some because it's the only work they can get. Between guild charity funds and the duke, they're paid a decent wage. Some cared once, but they've seen so much poverty that their hearts broke."

There was a sobering thought, Briar reflected, that you could love something and lose that love. Would he ever run out of love for green things? He brushed Rosethorn's sleeve with his fingertips so lightly that she didn't feel it.

No, he thought with a smile. I'll never run out of that.

They passed the second-floor landing and the ground floor, ducking around people who carried supplies upstairs. At last they came to a vast cellar. This floor too was busy: storerooms of all kinds lined one side of a stone-walled corridor. Opposite them were the furnace and pump rooms that got water to the wards.

Rosethorn headed straight to the last storeroom and entered. Briar, following, saw a large, brightly lit chamber lined from ceiling to floor with shelves. More racks of tall, freestanding shelves covered the floor. Jars of medicines sat on them, each container bearing a light coating of dust.

"One of their people—who fled two days ago— sold all the medicines I brought here over the last eighteen months," said Rosethorn, surveying the jars. "*And* the medicines I freshened up when I visited. Here's what's left, and it's more than a year old. If I could find her I would . . . well, never mind. This is what we have. You and I will restore or add as much virtue as we can to every shred and drop."

Briar's heart sank as he looked at all the shelves. "Can't somebody else do it?"

"Not like we can." Rosethorn took fat pottery jars marked *Willowbark* from the shelves closest to her and placed them on a workbench at the front of the room.

"Can we just get fresh from home?" asked Briar. This looked to be a long, dull, thankless chore.

"The whole city wants fresh medicines. Do you think Urda's House is at the top of the Lord Mayor's list?" Rosethorn shook her head. "Stop dancing, and get to work."

Picking up a knife from the workbench, Briar used it to break wax seals and pry the stoppers from the jars. The bark inside was dry, brittle, and scentless. "This is more than a year old," he announced, testing the bark with his magic, trying to judge how long it had been parted from its trees. "Like maybe two years."

"Of course it is," Rosethorn said. The sarcasm in her voice was not for him. "Why should this task have anything easy about it?" She yanked two large baskets from under the worktable, one for each of them. "Dump the jars into these—we'll do more if we go by basket instead of jar."

Once the baskets were full, Rosethorn lowered herself to the floor in a tailor's seat. "What we do is become the queen tree, the one from which all other willows are born—"

"Is there such a queen?" Briar asked, intrigued.

Rosethorn gave him a stern look. "The willows believe it, and they're the ones that matter. May I continue?" Briar nodded. She gave him an extra moment, just to be sure, then resumed. "Our magic will be the queen's sap that we put into this bark, to make it young and strong again."

She removed a vial from her pocket. It held the oil he called "Weigh anchor," because it was used to get a magical working started; Rosethorn named it "Facilitator." She had taught him to blend carnation, lotus, and myrrh oils in just the right way, so their powers of strength, purification, and the penetration of obstacles were at their height. She had even given him a rare compliment on his most recent batch, telling him she could feel it from across the room. Now, knowing what came next, he offered his hands.

She put a drop at the center of each palm, a third between his eyes. He felt them like tiny suns, their strength mingling with the magic in his blood. Rosethorn did the same to herself, then drew her basket onto her lap, steadying it with her oiled palms. Briar sat on the floor, his legs to either side of his own basket, placed his hands flat on the sides, then closed his eyes.

She towered in his mind's vision. He'd forgotten how it had taken his breath to see the tree-giant she was inside her pearly skin. He was stunned now, awed and a little frightened.

He touched her knee with his foot and mind-spoke: *You're like a giant* shakkan, *with all that power in you.*

Tend your bark, she ordered him, not unamused.

Briar drew away and thought about his own magic. So he was a queen willow now, was he? Better to be a *king* willow, he thought privately, trying to see it. Inch by inch he shaped himself: pale heartwood, gray bark riddled with fissures, long and wistful branches, lance-point leaves. His power shaped him and made the veins in his leaves shimmer. The basket turned as clear as fine glass to his power; he settled himself in its contents, feeding the dry, weak bark as if it were his own.

Enough. Rosethorn had touched his arm to speak to him. *Hold the tree in your mind, but release this load of bark. We have more to feed.*

He drew himself in, opened his eyes, and checked the basket. Its contents shimmered in his vision as they would have had they just been cut from strong trees.

Not too shabby, he told himself. Careful to hold the king willow in his mind, not letting its image break apart, he filled the jars he had emptied. I can do this, easy.

He and Rosethorn worked on four baskets each, renewing the bark's power to banish fever and pain, then returning it to the jars for use. When they had revived it all, Briar examined the king willow. For a moment he'd wondered how it would be to sink roots and sprout leaves. The idea was tempting, a way to escape this house, with its smells and cross people and the dying. A way to sit alone and love the sun.

Fighting the willow's pull, Briar looked around. Someone had left them a tray with a teapot, cups, bread, and a thick wedge of cheese.

"Food!" he said gleefully. The king willow's temptation evaporated. "Ain't soup neither!"

"It *isn't* soup *either*," Rosethorn corrected him wearily. She struggled to her feet. "I hope there's honey somewhere. I need it."

There was honey. Briar added plenty to the tea and watched sharp-eyed as she drank it, then gave her bread and cheese. Satisfied that she was eating, he gulped down his share of everything. When they'd finished, he felt just as fine as rubies.

"Say, Rosethorn?"

She stared at the bread in her fingers as if it were sawdust. "What?"

"When's your birthday?" It had come to him between willow baskets. To have the same birthday as Rosethorn—that would satisfy even Lady Sandrilene.

Rosethorn smiled crookedly. "Longnight."

He blinked at her. That couldn't be. *"Longnight?"* It was the hammer of winter, the night when all fires were doused and everyone prayed for the sun to rise.

She nodded, her smile twisted. "Doesn't that put

paid to those who claim our birthdates determine our lives? What kind of plant mage has a birthday on the longest night of the year?" Rosethorn sighed. "I celebrate at Midsummer instead—though not too much, as I get older. Who wants to be reminded of birthdays?" Raising her slender brows, she asked wickedly, "Still haven't picked one, boy?"

Briar shook his head gloomily.

"Well, don't look to me for help. Mine was the gods' own little joke. Now, where were we?"

Next came wild cherry bark, as dried up and stale as the willow. After three baskets each of that, Briar felt a little tired, but not enough to stop, not when he saw the shadows under Rosethorn's eyes. Instead he kept at it and gave lost vigor to coltsfoot, catnip, and plantain, all remedies for coughs or fever. Coming out of his trance after waking a basketful of red clover, he discovered Rosethorn was missing. He found her in the farthest corner of the room, her back to him and her hands over her face. Rosethorn—who terrified most of those with sense and everyone without it— was crying. Worse, she wept in the soft, dull way that meant she'd been at it for a while.

He wrapped his arms fiercely around her waist, resting his cheek on her back. "I'll find that light-fingered woman if I have to turn over every rock between here and the Bight of Fire," he whispered passionately. "Wherever she took the coin she got from selling your medicines, it ain't far enough to dodge *me*. I'll cut her in bitty chunks for you, would you like that? You could grill her over a fire and then feed her to sharks, like you always threaten me. Wouldn't that be fun?"

"I'm sorry," Rosethorn whispered. "I didn't mean to do this."

To hear her apologize for a fit of weeps just as the girls did nearly broke his heart. He'd never guessed how much of himself he'd tacked to Rosethorn, who feared nothing and nobody. "I'll give you her skin for a drape," he offered. "Just tell me, and I'll do it, I'll bring you her nicking fingers in pickle juice. I—"

"No," she said, trying to smile as she turned to face him. "It's not this—chore. Though I hate being down here without even a window, among all this, this *mast*." The word meant the litter of leaves, bark, and twigs that lay on the ground in the forest; it startled him that she used it to refer to the contents of these jars. She wiped her face on her arm, smearing the dust on her cheeks.

"Where's your handkerchief?" Briar asked.

Rosethorn shrugged.

He undid the strings that held her mask and wiped her cheeks with it. Her skin was dry and slack, he noted. Even her lips were pale. She looked—the best word he could think of was "shadowed."

Shadowed, he thought again, an idea tickling his brain. She feels like a plant in the shade.

He stepped back from her. Had there ever been a

day when she had not gone outside? He had run to the Water Temple or the Earth Temple with her in the foulest rains, or just walked, following Winding Circle's spiral road all the way down to the Hub and back out again as they stopped to examine every sleeping patch of flowers and vegetables.

"Should we go on the roof?" he inquired.

Rosethorn shook her head. "I'm not wilting for lack of sun, boy," she informed him.

He wasn't convinced she was right about that, not entirely.

Tears began to roll down her cheeks again. "Oh, dear," she whispered, turning her face away. "I want to be *home*," she said, almost to herself. "With Lark and the girls and even that idiot dog. I want people to stop—gabbling at me. I want my own workshop, and my own garden."

"I gabble at you," Briar pointed out softly.

"You don't," she said, once more wiping her face on her sleeve. "Not about cost, or when at the latest you have to get what you want. You aren't telling me to obey you or make things clear to someone or do written reports every day. You don't cough on me or vomit on me. . . ." She took a deep breath. "I wouldn't be weepy if I weren't tired. And if you ever tell *anyone* I got foolish like this, I'll deny it," she added, trying to sound like the Rosethorn he knew.

Briar reached out for the girls. Who at home was free? Not Sandry; she and Lark were rubbing oil into a length of undyed cotton like that used for masks and gloves. Not Daja either; she was helping Frostpine pour molten iron into a mold. Tris sat in Rosethorn's workshop, a book open before her, staring glumly out the window as rain streamed down outside.

Tris? Briar called silently to her. *I need my* shakkan *brought here right away—that and some of the potted herbs growing in the house. Living plants, mind.*

You want me to come all the way down there with a load of plants? was the redhead's indignant reply. *On a day like* this? She waved at the rainswept garden.

Please, he replied solemnly. *It's important.*

She reached back along their bond, feeling his distress, and looked at Rosethorn through him. If she noticed the tearstains or the bleak expression in Rosethorn's eyes, for once Tris was diplomatic enough to keep silent. *Oh, all right,* she said, exaggeratedly patient. *It's not like I have too much to do.*

Briar turned to Rosethorn. His silent chat with Tris had come and gone in a flash. "Look, we're both wore out. We did enough to hold them for an hour, I bet. So let's catch us some winks now, what do you say? I'll do it if you will."

She gripped his earlobe. "Street slang," she remarked.

"You're right, it is," he said blithely. "How 'bout them winks?"

"Are you trying to look after me?" she wanted to know.

97

Rather than answer so tricky a question, Briar yawned. Rosethorn's eyelids fluttered. "We should do more," she said, her voice soft. She fell silent, deep in thought, and Briar went to borrow two blankets from another storeroom. When he returned, she was curled up in a corner, already napping. Gently he covered her. It was cold in the cellar. He wrapped the second blanket around his own shoulders and took down jars of stale blackberry syrup for stomach ailments.

When Briar realized that his *shakkan* was somewhere near, he got to his feet. Rosethorn was still asleep; she had been up often in the night, trying to help the consumptive man. Briar put aside blanket and syrup and left the cellar. Halfway up the stairs, he remembered his cloth mask and settled it over his nose and mouth.

"Goods coming in," someone at the front door was shouting. "All back. Back!"

I'm here, Briar heard Tris say in mind-speech. *I hitched a ride with supplies from Winding Circle. The carter was only allowed to put everything onto the house porch, though, and they're making us go outside the fence. I won't even get to see you, will I?*

Dunno, Briar told her sadly. *Prob'ly not.*

Quarantined members of the Duke's Guard kept the sick who were able to walk away from the door. Two blue-robed healers went outside, a blinding shield of white light raised before them like a wall.

"Will that stuff hurt what I have coming in?" Briar asked Jokubas Atwater.

The man scowled at Briar. "This is not your affair," snapped the head of Urda's House. "Get back to bed where you belong."

"That's no invalid," said one of the guards. "That's Briar, Rosethorn's boy." He winked at Briar, taking the sting out of Jokubas's behavior. "She's got things coming in, lad?"

Briar nodded. "Plants."

"The cleansing spell will not hurt plants," Jokubas said irritably. "I thought you and she were enhancing our medicines."

"We are," Briar said evenly, without another word. The white light ahead of the two healers trickled around and through a pile of crates, baskets, and a lone wicker container without a top.

That's it, Tris told Briar, watching through his eyes. *I just grabbed what looked sturdy enough to survive the trip.*

When house staff walked out to get the supplies, Briar did too. The moment he peered into the basket, his spirits rose. Whether by accident or because she'd learned something from Briar and Rosethorn over the long winter, Tris had chosen plants Briar himself might have picked. The basket held not only his *shakkan*, but also one of Discipline's many protective ivy plants. Tris had even brought the small herb garden from the windowsill of Rosethorn's shop: marjoram, oregano, fennel, dill, and spearmint. All possessed some property of healing or protection in addition to the flavors they gave to food.

You done good, Coppercurls, Briar called out silently to Tris, who was climbing into the wagon for the trip home. *I owe you.*

Piffle, she replied, warmly pleased. *Like I said, I'm not exactly busy.*

Briar carried the basket downstairs very carefully. Without rousing his teacher, he arranged the plants around her curled-up form and waited.

After a minute or two color returned to her skin, changing ashen to cream. Her lips bloomed from white to pink. Her hair, which had looked brown over the last few days, developed a chestnut glow.

It was like she was dead, he realized with a shudder. Like she was dead, and somehow brought back to life.

Her eyes opened. They were slightly bloodshot yet, but their shine was back. She yawned widely. "Strike me for a ninny," she remarked, sitting up. She slid one hand around the *shakkan*'s trunk and cupped the ivy's bowl in the other. "It never once occurred to me that this was the problem."

"Me neither, till you said that about you not being a plant that needs sun," he said. "You never been in quarantine before, right?"

"I *have* never been in quarantine, yes," she said tartly.

Briar grinned, unrepentant. This was the Rosethorn he knew. She'd threaten a horrible death for someone any minute now.

"I'm always shut in with Crane, developing a cure. I never thought there'd come a day when I'd wish for that." She sighed. "We should get back to work."

Briar nodded and fetched more stale medicines for them to tend. Rosethorn sat for another moment, cradling each plant in her hands and tickling her face with the fronds.

As a plant mage, Rosethorn could tap the *shakkan*'s magical reserves, once Briar talked the tree into allowing it. For reasons that baffled the boy, the *shakkan* preferred his touch to Rosethorn's. With its help, and with Rosethorn's and even Briar's energies renewed by contact with living plants, they finished the job.

When done, they carried the potted plants upstairs in a basket.

"Let's share the wealth," Rosethorn suggested. "Give people something to look at." They left all of the plants but the *shakkan* on windowsills in the first- and second-floor wards. While Briar was glad to bring cheer to those rooms, he was unpleasantly surprised by how many people were in them. Each first-floor ward held thirty people, like their own upstairs. The three second-floor infirmaries were full, with a hundred patients in each. Adding in the first- and

101

third-floor wards, he realized that Urda's House contained nearly five hundred sick.

"Where are they coming from?" he asked Rosethorn as they took the empty basket to the first floor to be reused. He carried his *shakkan* in his arms; it would stay with him. "Are they all from the Mire?"

Rosethorn shook her head. A pile of empty crates and baskets lay beside the front door: she placed theirs on it. "We've been getting people from East District since yesterday. There's talk of emptying the houses on either side of this one to use them for quarantine."

"Not necessary," said a familiar voice. Both Rosethorn and Briar gasped as Niko walked out of a nearby office with Dedicate Henna and Jokubas Atwater. Niko wore not only gloves and mask, but also a long overrobe spelled so powerfully against disease that it made Briar's eyes smart to look at him. "With the plague now loose in the city, the Water Temple there has opened its normal hospital wards to take in those with blue pox."

"There's plague outside the East District?" asked Rosethorn.

"Ten cases this morning in Fountain Square," Niko replied, "and seven in Emerald Triangle."

Briar bit his lip. Niko had just named the two wealthiest districts inside the walls, where rich merchants and nobles lived. If the Money-Bags have it, everyone does, thought the boy.

"The duke is clearing an Arsenal warehouse for use as a hospital," Henna added. "I'm leaving to get things set up there."

"What about the quarantine?" asked Briar.

"It's over, isn't it?" Rosethorn asked Niko and Jokubas. "There's no point anymore, not with cases throughout Summersea."

Both men nodded.

Briar yipped with glee. "Then we can go home!"

"No," said all four adults at once, startling him.

"Why not?" he demanded, suddenly furious. What good was he doing here, and why shouldn't he leave? They had plenty of healers now. He wanted his own room, in his own house, and food cooked by the peerless Gorse in temple kitchens. He wanted Lark to say how brave he'd been and to hear the Hub clock sound the hours. Open air would be nice, and proper sun, and a roll on the grass with his dog. He could settle back among the girls, where he belonged.

Who would look after Flick? asked a quiet voice within him. Does anyone care about her but you?

Rosethorn put an arm around Briar's shoulder. "There's no disease at Winding Circle," she explained softly. "Is there?" She put the question directly to Niko, who shook his head. "Until we know how this plague is carried, we can't risk taking the blue pox uphill to our friends."

"But *you're* going back, ain't you?" Briar demanded of Niko.

"Yes, I am," snapped the mage. "I also have to stop at a tent outside the Mire, get rid of my clothes, scrub every inch with a vile soap that makes me itch, then rub in an even more vile-smelling oil before I can leave. If I thought you did more good at Winding Circle than here, I would be quite pleased to suggest that you get the same."

Briar glared at Niko, who glared right back. If he'd been feeling tolerant, Briar would have seen that Niko's eyes were tired, his skin chapped and red, and backed off. Briar was not feeling tolerant just then.

"This reeks!" he yelled, terrified that he would spend the rest of his life in Urda's House. "This really, really reeks! Lakik's mercy to the blue pox and whatever sent it!" He ran upstairs with his *shakkan*, fighting the urge to cry like a baby. The problem was that he was already seeing Lakik's mercy, which was no mercy at all.

Frostpine placed the lid on a sample box; Daja gave it one last rub. Kirel took it to the girl in the yellow habit of the Air Temple who waited in the doorway. She balanced a wooden crate nearly filled with sample boxes in a wheelbarrow. Kirel placed his burden there, shut the crate, and fastened the leather strap that kept the lid on. The girl thanked him, giving the big youth a sidelong glance, then turned the wheelbarrow and trundled it away.

"Perhaps you should help her," Frostpine suggested as he winked at Daja. "She looked strong, but such loads are delicate. . . ."

Daja noticed that Kirel's skin turned a nice shade of crimson. "She seemed to like you," she pointed out, massaging her fingers.

"I'll see her at supper," Kirel replied. "Her and her girlfriends eat at a table close to mine." He brushed his white habit, trying to wipe away soot marks.

"Are your hands all right?" Frostpine asked Daja, putting away the rest of his tools. "I know engraving is hard, but you did so well that I didn't think to ask."

Daja tucked her hands into her tunic pockets. "I'm just surprised they're empty," she said. "How many days have we been at this?"

"I lost track," Kirel remarked wearily. He ladled water from the barrel and poured it over his long braids, blowing like a whale.

Frostpine slung one arm around Kirel's wet shoulders and another around Daja's. "You did fine work," he told his students. "Only the healers, and Lark and Sandry, are working harder." He let them go. "Daja, my pearl, you can return to Discipline tonight, if you like."

"I would," Daja replied. "Did we make enough of those things?"

"They have enough to last a month, and tomorrow we are going to rest," Frostpine announced as they went outside.

"Here! Watch it!" cried a man just when they would have walked onto the spiral road. Four wagons rolled by, each carrying novices and Fire and Earth Temple dedicates. They were armed with picks and shovels. Still more wagons followed, laden with canvas, empty carry-baskets, and lumber.

"What's all this?" Frostpine asked one of the drivers.

"Setting up a hospital camp," replied the woman, an Earth Temple dedicate. "Hospital camp and an open pit for burning the dead." When Frostpine and his students stared at her in shock, she said, "Where have you been? The blue pox is everywhere in the city. Urda's House and the Water Temple are full up. Duke's clearing a warehouse, and they're building the camp uphill of the Mire. Pit's to be dug on Bit Island." Her wagon rolled on, bound for the south gate and the road to the city.

Briar? asked Daja, reaching through their magical connection. *Are you all right?* She was suddenly frightened for him and Rosethorn.

I'm fine. Go away, Briar replied firmly. Daja was cut off as crisply as if he'd slammed a door in her face.

As Briar stalked down the hall to the room where Flick was, a healer stopped him. "Mask, gloves," he said tiredly. "We've fresh ones on the tables; use them."

Briar wanted to tell him off as he'd just told Daja, but the man looked so weary over his own mask that Briar decided it wasn't worth it. He put the *shakkan* down and helped himself to a mask. A sense of Lark and Sandry washed over him as herb-scented cloth pressed his nose. He could almost see their faces, their magic was so powerfully written into the undyed cotton. The gloves were the same. Fitting them over his hands, he felt as if Lark and Sandry stood at his back, keeping him safe.

That made him feel small.

Daj'? he called out silently, sheepishly. *Daj', I'm sorry.*

He could feel the Trader's hurt, as sharp as if he'd cut her. Then Daja too relaxed. *It's bad there?*

Bad enough, he replied, stroking the *shakkan's* wrinkled trunk. *Ain't you heard?*

Only a bit, just now, she told him somberly. *We've been making sample boxes 'round the clock, with breaks for catnaps.*

She felt exhausted to him. Now he was *really* ashamed of himself. *Sleep and eat,* he told her sternly. *Lots of both.*

One epidemic and you're a master healer? she asked, amusement threading her weariness.

That's it, he agreed, mock-serious. *Tell them at home me and Rosethorn miss 'em.*

I will, she replied, drawing away.

Feeling better for the contact, Briar carried his tree into the ward he'd left that morning. His bed had been filled.

"You aren't sick," replied a healer when he protested. "You shouldn't be here."

Briar settled his tree on the shelf behind Flick's cot. "I should be and I am," he said firmly. "I'll see to my—my mate, here." The term wasn't strictly accurate: a mate was someone who stayed with you in dire times, as the girls had with him the year before. Still, he was as much of a mate as Flick was going to get. Lifting his eyebrows, he asked, "You want to argue?"

"Just keep out of my way," the man warned him, moving on to other beds.

That was easy enough. Flick had sunk into a high fever while Briar was out. He checked her mouth, to find her tongue as dry as paper. Her cracked lips bled; her skin was ashy and dry. When he pinched her gently, the fold he'd made in her skin flattened very slowly. He'd been around healers enough to know this was the worst possible sign. His friend was drying up inside.

His heart pounded heavily. What was going on here? He'd thought she was on the mend that morning. Looking around, he saw that the homeless man Yuvosh was gone. A kid Henna had brought in and one of her old people were missing too.

"Dead," said a healer—not the one who'd told him he didn't belong there—when he asked. "Yuvosh, did you say his name was?—had a stroke. The old woman in her sleep; her heart stopped. It was quick. The little boy went into a coma and died—fever cooked his brain. Your girl started to heat up about an hour after you left. You won't be able to give her enough liquid to make a difference," she added as Briar grabbed a clean jar and filled it with water.

"We'll see," he said grimly, filling a smaller jar with willowbark tea. He marched back to the bed, determined to do battle. Flick's response was not encouraging: she swallowed two mouthfuls and let the rest dribble onto her blanket.

"Open your eyes," Briar ordered, trying to sit her up. "C'mon, Flick, you're drier than the rooftops in Wort Moon. You *have* to drink."

Flick's eyes popped open. "Ma, don't!" she cried, raising her hands against an unseen threat. "I'll learn, I will, only *don't*—" Her head snapped back. She keened deep in her throat and curled into a ball. "I'll be good. I'll be good," she whispered, sobbing.

"Flick, drink this," Briar said, badly frightened. "I know it's nasty, but it'll help."

Flick sat up with a grin. "There's a haul, and proper nicked!" she sang out. "And food enough for everybody after the Dirt Mayor gets his cut."

Briar got the cup to her mouth and tipped it, pouring half down her throat. She drank, thinking it was part of the food she'd stolen in her waking dream. "Naw, give 'em dates to the littles," she announced. "Too bleatin' sweet for me. How 'bout some o' that wine, there."

Briar filled the cup from the water jar and raised it to her lips, but he was too late. Flick lay back, eyelids fluttering. "You want Petticoat to work the Bag trade. She's got the lingo. Gimme wharves any road." She slept briefly, her breath rasping in her dry throat, and woke to still more hallucinations. As the healers closed the shutters for the night and supper was brought to those who could eat, Briar learned more about Flick's early life than he ever wanted to. He wished, tiredly, that he could find the monstrous mother who figured so vividly in his friend's cries.

Worse, he wished that he'd never heard of Flick. He hoped that she would die so he could get some rest. That last thought made him despise himself. Her life was surely worth more than his winks. He was a monster to think it. As penance he fought her to drink more liquid. When she refused, he helped tend those on either side of her. One of them was Orji, the other homeless man who had come in that second day. He slept lightly, muttering in his dreams, but he drank when he was told, and he wasn't as hot as he'd been.

Just after the Guildhall clock struck midnight, Flick went stiff, her body turning into a bow. Just her head and feet touched the bed. She collapsed as Briar and a blue-robed healer ran to her cot, then arched again, unbreathing, eyes rolled up in her head.

"Get her feet!" snapped the healer. She threw her body across Flick, grabbing her wrists. While Briar

111

hung on to the girl's feet, the healer took a breath and exhaled. Her magic surged like fast-growing vines through Flick's arms and into her straining chest. Flick collapsed, gasping as she tried to suck air into her dry throat.

"Breathe," the healer urged Flick. "Breathe as hard as you—"

Flick whined. Her back arched as her eyes rolled up. Now the healer sent power racing through her, filling the girl's skin with magic only Briar could see. The magic's light fluttered; in Flick's arms and legs it receded, trickling back into her body almost as quickly as it had filled her limbs.

This time Flick's convulsion was shorter. "Breathe," chanted the healer softly when she went limp. "Breathe, breathe—"

Briar was confused. Why was it important for Flick to breathe? Wasn't it Henna—? Yes. She'd said that in long moments without air, parts of the brain died. People with seizures forgot to breathe. Urda, no, thought Briar, scowling at his friend. Don't leave her an idiot.

Flick tensed again. Two more seizures followed, the healer never once loosening her grip. Each time it took her more effort to thrust her magic into Flick's body, and it never lasted as long inside the girl's skin as it had the first time.

When Flick had lain quiet for a while, the healer

let go. Briar, who'd been knocked repeatedly into the bedstead, was happy to release the girl's feet.

"Could I do that?" he asked the healer as she gulped down cold water. "Put my magic in them to keep them going?"

"Are you a healer?" the woman asked tiredly. "Can you run your power through another human being?"

"Only my mates—these girls I know—and Rosethorn."

The healer looked at him—really looked—for the first time. "Yanna bless me, you're one of the four, aren't you? The boy, the plant-mage?" Briar nodded. The healer massaged her temples. "You might do it with those girls and Rosethorn, but we would have been told if any of you could heal."

"Could I try?" asked Briar as the healer lurched to her feet.

"Try all you like," she replied. "Nothing will come of it." She hesitated, then touched Flick's head. Once again Briar saw magic, but its gleam was just visible—the woman was nearly drained. She pursed her lips.

"Flick'll be fine," snapped Briar, annoyed by the healer's rejection of the idea that he could do this kind of magic.

"I hope so," she replied, moving on to the next bed.

Sitting beside his friend, Briar held her wrists as the healers did. Magic was magic. It could be lent to other mages; he'd seen that, had done it himself. Let him bleed off some now, when there was some good to be had.

His store of power wasn't the same as it had been that morning, before he and Rosethorn had gone downstairs, but he still had some. He pictured Flick's veins like veins in a leaf and urged his magic forward. It was like trying to leap off a cliff, only to find he was still on even ground. There was no place for him to go. Again he tried, imagining her veins as a web of roots. His power moved in him, but went nowhere.

A hand on his shoulder jolted Briar out of a half trance. "It doesn't work," Rosethorn said wryly. "I've tried. How has she been doing?"

Briar described Flick's seizures and the shrinking amounts of magic that the healer had fed to his friend. Rosethorn frowned as he spoke. When he was done, she said, "I'll be back shortly." She left him there.

"Can I have water?" Orji whispered from the next bed. "My head aches."

Briar scooped water into a cup and helped raise the man so he could drink. Looking for Rosethorn as Orji gulped the water, Briar saw her arguing softly—but ferociously, from the look on her face—with the healer who'd tended Flick. The healer pointed to other cots and shook her head. Was she telling Rosethorn she'd already helped those people and was drained of magic, or was she saying there were others who needed it more than Flick?

It didn't matter, decided Briar. She wouldn't help Flick, if she even could. The healer's shoulders drooped; she leaned on the table as she argued with Rosethorn—she was nearly played out. Finally Rosethorn left the room. Briar returned to his watch over Flick.

Some time after the Guildhall clock struck one, Flick passed into unmoving sleep. The clock was ringing the half hour after three in the morning when the consumptive man began to cough himself to death, noisily and bloodily. Orji tried to stuff his blanket into his ears to escape the sound. Briar trembled, wishing he could do the same. Suddenly the noise ended. Those in the room who were able to understand made the gods-circle on their chests.

Flick slept through it all, unmoving, her breath rattling in her throat. Briar tried to get her to drink tea or water, but it ran from her loose mouth. "You have to get well," he told her fiercely. "C'mon, Flick. You're a *fighter*. Remember that time we was on the wharf and them Trader boys tried to run us off?" Tris, Sandry, and Daja knew of this adventure, but their teachers did not. "We showed 'em, right? You even got a fine cloth cap out of it. Sky blue, with a peacock feather, and the pump we saw told you it was worth three silver crescents."

Flick's breathing slowed, as if she *did* remember. As if she savored the memory of either the victory or the hat.

115

Cheered by that, Briar talked on. "Once we're sprung from here, I'll ask Sandry to make a cape to go with the hat, same color and everything." He was breathing along with Flick, though he didn't realize it at first. Her body clawed for air like a weary fisherman hauling in nets a handful at a time. There was always a halt when Flick stopped inhaling. Each time Briar stopped when she did. Waiting longer and longer for her to start again, he silently begged her to let go of her lungfuls of air. He couldn't talk as well as breathe with her, to help her, so he shut up and clutched her hand, watching her chest slowly rise— and fall. Rise—and fall.

Rise . . . and fall.

Rise . . . rise . . . fall. Fall.

He emptied his chest and waited. She was about to breathe in, about to at any minute, except, except . . .

Briar choked and gasped, inhaling frantically to fill starved lungs. He wheezed as spittle went into his airway, then coughed and coughed, until he yanked the mask from his mouth and drank water straight from the jar. When he lowered it, Flick still hadn't moved, hadn't filled her lungs.

She had lost so much weight. A skeleton with skin, he thought, taking her hand again. When she got better, he would try to talk Winding Circle into taking her. Gorse, the chief cook, would love to bring her to a proper weight. Gorse *lived* to feed people.

Someone fumbled with his hands, but he wouldn't

let go of her. After a time they went away. Briar sat, thinking of the mischief they would find once Flick was on her feet.

Fingers of light thrust through a crack in the shutters, telling him it was dawn. Flick would ask for breakfast in a little while.

A finger touched him lightly, between the eyes. In his mind he saw a silver ribbon of magic. His nostrils flared, tickled by a scent of patchouli, lotus, and other things.

"Red as blood," a man remarked. "You can take him home, Dedicate."

"Briar." Hands cupped his cheeks and turned his head. His eyes met Rosethorn's.

"Why is there a red thumbprint on your face?" he asked.

"It's Crane's detection oil. If you have the blue pox, it turns white on your skin. If not, it turns red. Yours is red, mine is red, and we're going home." She seemed to be pleading with him; her tone was gentle.

"If I get up I'll wake Flick," he pointed out, not unreasonably, he thought.

"My dear, you know better," Rosethorn said. Her brown eyes were level, serious. There was no pity in them. He was glad. Pity would have hurt.

Briar looked at his friend. Her fingers were limp in his, her mouth was slack. No pulse beat in the thin skin over her temple. She was just a shell, lying there.

Silently Briar pulled his hand away. He picked up

117

his *shakkan*, then followed Rosethorn out of the ward.

Quarantine had lifted, but no one was taking chances. Once they were out of Urda's House, they entered the tent that Niko had mentioned, the one beside the road to Winding Circle. There the clothes they'd worn were taken away while they scrubbed with medicinal soap, rinsed in hot water, and rubbed themselves in disinfectant oil. When they emerged, they were handed fresh clothing. Briar examined the folded garments and realized these were his own, from Discipline. His eyes blurred; he opened them wide, so no one might see rinse water on his face and mistake it for tears. He dressed, pulling on his second favorite boots. His favorites, he remembered, were gone, destroyed on his first day at Urda's House as part of the useless attempt to keep the disease from spreading.

A squad of the Duke's Guard mounted on horses awaited them in front of the tent.

"We're to give you a ride to Winding Circle," their corporal told Rosethorn. "Honored Moonstream asked us, if you turned out to be well."

"I don't have the blue pox," Rosethorn said bleakly. "I don't know if I'm well."

The mounts picked their way along Nosegay Strut, the street that ran past Urda's House to Temple Road and the fishing village on the harbor. Briar looked around dully. The day he'd come here with nothing more on his mind than unloading medicines and running about with Flick, the street had been muddy but clear. Now it was strewn with the remains of bonfires, pieces of wood, liquor bottles, and trash. There were heaps of rags: the dead, left to be picked up by the big vehicles mockingly called lumber wagons. Three buildings showed signs of fire; another had burned to the ground. Drunkards and beggars leaned on buildings and watched as the guards passed. Doors and window shutters slammed all around.

It began to rain as they turned onto Temple Road. On the north edge of the way, several houses had burned; on the south edge, the fishing village had built a wall of barrels and wagons to keep rioters from their boats. As the road climbed into rocky ground, he saw men and women in street clothes and habits already hard at work. They were putting down plank floors and raising large canvas tents. Three or four giant tents were already taking in the sick: the guards had to swing around a line of wagons carrying fresh victims to the makeshift hospitals.

A heavy, cooked-meat smell drifted into his nose as the wind whipped around. From Bit Island a thick black trunk of smoke rose to mark where the dead were burned.

The guards watched their surroundings, though nothing lay now to their right except the bluffs and, below them, the slate-gray waters of the harbor. To their left rose tumbled earth, giant slabs of rock, and whatever plants could get a foothold on such un-promising ground. The greenery drew Briar's eyes; he touched the *shakkan* he carried in the crook of one arm.

"I forgot the plants at Urda's House!" he gasped suddenly. "Rosethorn—"

"They need them more than we do," she replied. "Don't worry about it."

He dozed, tucked so firmly behind his guard that he couldn't fall. He woke suddenly: an animal was screaming. Leaning to look around the guard, he saw that they had reached a Y in the road, where it split to either side of a well and a shrine. He knew both. Higher on the rising ground soared gray stone walls. Atop them, warriors in red habits and broad-brimmed hats against the rain leaned through notches to stare at them.

Down the road that led to Winding Circle's north gate raced the screeching animal: a big white dog nearly out of his mind with joy. Behind him came Daja, walking sensibly on the firm ground at the road's edge, using her staff to keep herself out of the mud. Tris followed her, raising her skirts as she picked her way past the worst ruts and dips in the road itself. Last came Lark and Sandry under a big umbrella the same earth-green shade as Lark's habit.

Briar's guard commented, amused, "I see there's a welcoming committee."

Little Bear reached them first, sending up gouts of

muddy water as he raced from Briar's horse to Rosethorn's. No one tried to speak; none of them could have heard anything but the dog.

Daja stopped by Rosethorn, looking up at her. After a moment she smiled, carefully, as if she were unsure Rosethorn would like it. Briar saw his teacher reach down and wrap her fingers around the Trader's dark hand where she clutched her staff. Daja's smile broadened, and Rosethorn let go.

Daja came over to Briar, staying clear of Little Bear. Briar looked at her, seeing that she was still tired after long hours in the forge. She gazed up at him for a long moment, then said, "You took your time coming home, thief-boy."

Briar felt his guard stiffen. He tried to smile. "I woulda been home sooner, if I'd had my druthers."

Tris only glanced up at Rosethorn and nodded, turning pink as she did. Rosethorn nodded back. When the redheaded girl reached Briar, she said frankly, "You look like you were eaten by wolves."

"Nothing so nice," he replied, and carefully handed the *shakkan* down to her.

Half turning in the saddle, his guard asked, "You're leaving me already?"

Briar nodded. "I must. These girls will just get weepy and embarrass me if you stay." He slid into the road, landing to one side of a puddle. Daja steadied him.

Sandry closed the distance between them at a run.

Colliding with him, she wrapped her arms tightly around his neck. "You dreadful boy!" she cried. "Don't you *ever* do that again!"

He patted her awkwardly and growled, "You're making my shirt wet, crying on it."

Sandry laughed and stood back, wiping her eyes. "It's already soaked through. Tris, can't you deal with all this rain?" She fumbled in her pockets until she found her handkerchief.

"Why is it always me?" asked the redhead without expecting a reply. A circle of dry air opened around the entire group, rain streaming to all sides as if she'd covered them with a glass bowl. The guards glanced at each other sidelong, unnerved by the display of magic. Tris didn't even notice.

Sandry blew her small nose briskly and inspected Briar once she'd put the linen handerchief away. "You need rest, and you need decent food," she announced. "Rosethorn probably hasn't done much better than you."

"Look for yourself," Daja remarked softly. Sandry turned.

Rosethorn had dismounted. Now she stood ankle deep in mud, arms wrapped tight around Lark, her face buried in Lark's shoulder as the other woman held her. She didn't seem to be crying; she just hung onto her friend for all she was worth.

Sandry gathered her skirts and went over to the women, sliding her own arms around Rosethorn's waist. Daja followed her more slowly, to pat Rosethorn's back. Briar went to stand nearby. Tris, crimson with emotion, glared at the guards as if daring them to comment.

Their corporal twitched his head. Quietly they turned their mounts and rode back to Summersea.

When Rosethorn drew out of Lark's and Sandry's holds, she said crossly, "I'm not crying, if that's what you're thinking. I'm just . . . tired. I needed to rest for a moment."

Lark wrapped an arm around her shoulders. "No wonder. You two look worn to the bone, my dearest. And why not? Locked up for days, like jail, without your garden and only nursing to occupy you—I think Little Bear likes nursing more than you." She drew Rosethorn uphill, toward Winding Circle. The four and Little Bear walked along. Lark continued, "And I bet Jokubas and his people were talking at you too."

"As if this were my fault," Rosethorn said blackly, and sniffed.

"But you're all right now," Sandry announced. "You're both home safe, and we're going to be fine."

"The epidemic is far from over," cautioned Lark. "We still have work."

"But we're where we should be. That's the important thing," Sandry replied cheerfully. "We're all *home.*"

Soon after Rosethorn's and Briar's return, everyone but Tris went back to bed: Daja was exhausted from her work in the forge, Lark and Sandry from spelling cloth to keep disease at bay. Not long after they went to their rooms, novices came with fresh supplies of oils, powders, and clothing. Tris directed them to Lark's workshop and watched as they placed their supplies along the wall. She noticed that the big makeshift table in the workshop had to be scrubbed, the wood cleaned of anything from the day before. Tris did that first; it was the only thing she could help them with. The dull work of blending fresh ingredients into a paste that blazed with magical strength, then rubbing it into cloth, was Lark's and Sandry's craft.

Once the table was clean, scrubbed with sand, and wiped down with an infusion of thyme leaves, Tris checked the cold-box. Rosethorn's and Briar's arrival had caught her by surprise. Until now Lark and Sandry had been too weary to eat anything but soup at the end of the day, and Daja had taken her meals with Frostpine and Kirel. Tris didn't have the supplies she needed to feed the entire cottage again. Picking up two baskets, she walked out onto the spiral road that wound through the temple community. It would take her to the central kitchens at the Hub.

On her way back to Discipline, Tris didn't realize she had company until long hands wrapped around one of her baskets and tugged. Looking up with a sharp comment ready for the interloper, she saw Dedicate Crane.

She surrendered the basket without an argument. Work was good for Crane. "You look *terrible*," she informed him. "And doesn't that wash off?" She pointed to the red thumbprint between his eyes. "Rosethorn and Briar still have theirs from this morning."

"I spelled it to last for weeks," Crane drawled. "It is better so, particularly when one is known to be exposed to the disease regularly. And I am sorry I do not meet your qualifications for male beauty. I have been working."

"You look like you need a rest," she replied. "It won't do anyone good to have you fall ill from overwork."

"You are too young to sound like my former governess," Crane informed her as they walked across the road to Discipline. Little Bear came bounding out, set to give Tris his usual hysterical greeting. When he saw her companion, the dog raced back inside. On his frequent visits to the cottage after he had asked for Lark's help, Crane had made his opinion of enthusiastic dogs very clear.

"They must be up," said Tris, allowing the man to open the gate for her. "Little Bear is sticking close to Briar."

"Fortunate Briar," murmured Crane as they went inside.

The cottage's inhabitants were seated at the table, clutching steaming cups of tea. Rosethorn's head came up when she saw Crane.

"Turn right back around," she said tartly. "I didn't escape quarantine to get buckled into *your* harness."

Tris took her basket from Crane and carried everything into the kitchen area. Sandry brought the man a chair from Lark's workroom.

"Charming as ever," Crane remarked as he arranged himself on the chair. "However did they manage to entertain you at Urda's House?"

"Only you could make 'Urda's House' sound like an ill wish," Rosethorn growled.

Crane raised a single eyebrow. "I would have to care about the place to ill wish it," he informed her. "I assume their own poor management is curse enough for them."

"How would you know about their management or anything else?" demanded Rosethorn. "You wouldn't sully the purity of your habit by going anywhere near the Mire."

"Shall I point out that your mission of mercy to the impoverished resulted in your enforced stay?" drawled Crane. "On second thought, I shall not. You so frequently assure me you are attentive to all things that I must believe you spent your last week in quarantine by design."

"Will you both just *stop*?" Lark asked wearily. "There's nothing to be gained by bickering." She smiled a thank you at Tris, who was setting bowls and plates on the table.

Sandry got up to help, but Tris waved her back into her seat. Within a few moments everyone was able to help themselves to the food sent by the temple's finest cooks.

When Rosethorn put down her fork, Crane said, "With regard to your time—"

"No!" Briar said hotly, glaring at Crane. "Let her be! Find somebody more important. She did her bit, and she needs rest!" When Rosethorn put a hand on his arm, he shook her off. "I know you swore to serve folk when you got dedicated," he told her, "but you got to be sensible, and if you won't speak up, I will." He glared at Crane, who regarded him as if he were a bug. "Find one of them *great* mages that's up to your weight," insisted the boy.

"'One of them great mages,'" Crane repeated tonelessly. "Are you serious?" He looked at each of the four, brows arched, mouth pursed. "None of you has the least notion, I take it?"

The young people stared at Lark, then Rosethorn, confused. Both women looked down, not meeting their charges' eyes.

Tris scowled at Crane. "The least notion of what?"

Crane sighed and fanned himself with a linen handkerchief. "Rosethorn *is* a great mage. She is one of the most powerful with regard to medicines and plants in all the Pebbled Sea and its environs."

"He says 'one of' because he means he's another," muttered Rosethorn. She poured herself a fresh cup of tea.

Crane sniffed. "Surely that is obvious." To the four he said, "Winding Circle is the rival of the university at Lightsbridge in the renown and quality of its mage-teachers. It is famed from Yanjing to Blaze-Ice Bay." He sighed. "You didn't know about Winding Circle either. How charming."

"We knew that Niko's a great mage," said Tris. "Someone we met last fall told us."

Crane inclined his head in agreement as regally as any king. "Lark too is a great mage, for all she came to it later in life," he went on. "Frostpine is the greatest of the smith-mages of our time. None other can work all kinds of metal, except for young Daja, here."

Briar, Sandry, and Tris looked at Daja, who shrugged. She had known of Frostpine's reputation for a year, but had not chosen to speak of it much. Frostpine wanted to teach her: nothing else mattered.

Crane went on, "You four have the honor of studying with teachers of royal magnitude. How you could be ignorant of their stature—"

The young people looked down, embarrassed.

"Oh, cork it," said Rosethorn, glaring at the man. "Don't belabor the point. It happens we are the best teachers for their talents—that's all they ever needed to know. If you have something really important to say, *say* it. I want to go back to bed."

Crane spread his handkerchief on the table and fussed with it, folding it into a series of tiny pleats. After a moment he said quietly, "Very well. Here it is, with no flourishes: most of those sent to work with me are hopeless. I have no time to both teach them and uncover the nature of this disease. You know this work must be done quickly and accurately, by masters, not green students."

"I'm so tired," Rosethorn muttered. She looked up, meeting Crane's eyes. "You don't need me. You have a diagnosis oil; you must be halfway to a cure."

"If I am, it is news to me," replied Crane acidly.

"Finding the oil was luck. As far as divining the heart of the disease, I have done test after test, without result." He took a deep breath. "We have our differences, but you know—I would hope you know—that I respect your gifts and your knowledge. You are needed."

Briar was uneasy, hearing so proud a man do what sounded too close to begging for comfort. He knew without even reaching out that the girls felt it too. He wanted to offer to help, but there was too much unpleasantness between him and Crane. In the man's eyes he was a low-bred thief—Briar did steal the *shakkan* from Crane's greenhouse—and in Briar's experience Money-Bags like Crane never changed their minds about people like him.

"I'll help." Rosethorn looked at Crane. "You knew I would."

Crane relaxed, giving something that sounded like a sigh of relief. "I thought you might want me to beg just a while longer."

"Once they stop fussing, they really do well together," Lark explained to the young people. With a glare at the other two adults she added, "They just have to get the fuss out of the way."

"She has no system," began Crane.

"He'd rather criticize how other people work," added Rosethorn.

"You see what I mean," Lark told the four.

"We've never handled a brand-new disease, though we know the theory," Crane pointed out quietly. "Finding cures for the current manifestation of old diseases is our strongest area of expertise."

"You tried all the procedures for known diseases?" Rosethorn asked suddenly. "The smallpox ones, and the measles ones? Just in case?"

Crane looked down his lofty nose. "You must be mistaking me for an apprentice," he told her coolly. "It was the first thing I did."

Rosethorn made a face. "All right. Speaking of apprentices—"

Crane looked at Briar. "No. Absolutely not."

"Absolutely yes," snapped Rosethorn as Briar glared at Crane. "You don't have to work with him—"

"I don't want him in my greenhouse."

"He's thorough, he does exactly what he's told, and he has the steadiest hands of anyone in Winding Circle," Rosethorn informed Crane.

Briar gaped at her. So much praise from Rosethorn was unnerving. Until the start of quarantine, he could count on his fingers the number of times she'd so much as said "Good job," and still have plenty of fingers left.

Crane raised his brows. "I know he possesses steady hands. He is a pickpocket."

"You're in no position to refuse," Rosethorn told him. "I need to know if he can do this. There are too few of us who have any aptitude for it. If he's one, we'll find out."

Crane sighed, and looked at Briar. "Keep out of my way," he warned, getting up.

Briar was about to spit on the floor to show his opinion of the man, but Rosethorn caught his eye. He didn't need to mind-speak with her to see the warning in her face.

Lark put out a hand to delay Crane's departure. "Sandry, the new masks and gloves." Sandry darted into their workroom as Lark asked Crane, "How are you on the spelled robes and foot covers?"

"We have enough for tomorrow and the day after," Crane replied. "I suppose we will need smaller ones, though, for the boy." He said it without looking at Briar.

Sandry returned with a metal box. She squinted as she handed it to Crane; the other three turned their faces away from the blaze of magic coming from the protections on the box and from its contents.

"What's the matter with them?" Crane wanted to know.

"They see magic," explained Lark. "Don't you?"

"No," Crane admitted. "I have a visualization potion I use when I need to see it, but I confess, it makes my skin break out. Rosethorn?"

She sighed. "I know. Dawn. Get some sleep."

Crane thanked Lark and walked out into the gray afternoon.

"I don't like him," Briar growled softly.

"You don't have to," said Rosethorn, getting to her feet with a yawn.

"I won't do it," retorted Briar. "I just won't."

Rosethorn lifted her own eyebrows, enough like Crane that Briar, who'd never seen a resemblance before now, blinked at her. "There are adult mages, rejoicing in great power and knowledge, who would *kill* for the chance to work for Dedicate Crane," she informed him. Then her mouth twitched. "Of course, they don't know him personally."

Sandry giggled.

"It won't kill either of us, though we may wish it had," said Rosethorn. "I'm going back to bed. So should you—we're due at the greenhouse first thing tomorrow."

Briar, about to argue, choked. He had been inside the Air Temple's greenhouse only once, to steal the *shakkan*. After that, he wasn't even allowed to loiter near it, to glimpse at the unknown plant-treasures inside.

"Oh, didn't I mention that?" asked Rosethorn, her voice a little too innocent. "Crane's workroom is inside the greenhouse." She sauntered into her room and closed the door.

"She must feel *some* better if she's tormenting people," said Lark, standing. "I'd better get to work." She walked into her workroom. Sandry followed and closed the door as Tris and Daja gathered the dishes.

He splashed through the sewers in a pure white novice's robe that was much too big for him. He wore nothing under it, and—to his shock and disgust—he was barefoot. His bare toes sank through inches of the kind of muck that made his guts crawl to think of it.

"Come *on*," ordered Flick. He saw her clearly, though neither of them carried lamps. "We'll miss your birthday party." She was properly dressed in rags and shoddy boots, jigging in her eagerness to move along.

Briar muttered about not having a birthday, let alone a party, but he followed as quickly as the habit would allow. She was moving farther off down the pipe. "Wait up!" he called, trying to lift the habit's skirts. Flick only laughed and ran on.

The tunnel bent around a corner. When he cleared it, Flick was nowhere in sight. "Hey!" he yelled. "Where'd you get to?"

Her laugh emerged from an opening several feet away. He followed the sound and saw Flick well ahead. "Wait!"

"Briar's gettin' slo-ow, Briar's gettin' slo-ow," she taunted. He sighed. She had done this just before the Longnight holiday, when he'd followed her through a warren of streets in the worst part of the Mire. She'd almost given him the slip then, just as now. He wasn't about to lose her, not down here.

The pipe shrank, forcing him to walk hunched over. With every step he took, she seemed to take three. "You got to slow down!" he cried.

"You got to speed up," she retorted, and giggled.

"Will you just *wait*?" he demanded. The filthy water rose, eddying around his calves, then his knees. It dragged on the habit, pulling him back.

"I can't, Briar," she said, voice somber. "I can't wait, even if it is your birthday."

"Flick!" he cried, battling water and habit to close with her. "Stop!"

The girl shrugged and ran off down the pipe. Briar watched in panic as she got farther and farther away. Something bad lay ahead. If he lost sight of her, it would be the end. He shucked the habit impatiently and pumped his suddenly weak legs, fighting to gain speed. He was too slow; she was too quick. She grew smaller and smaller.

"Flick!" he screamed, and she was gone. He was awake.

If his bed hadn't been a mattress on the floor, he might have fallen out. Instead Briar thrashed his way out of the covers that tangled around him. Little Bear whined and licked sweat off the boy's face. Panting, Briar sat out the shakes, clenching his hands as he remembered how he couldn't hold Flick, not in a dream, not in Urda's House. How could he have let her die, with all this magic to serve him? He didn't try hard enough—if he had, Flick would be alive. He'd as good as killed her himself by not doing more.

Sandry came in, which was only to be expected. Her bedroom was across from his. In one open palm she carried her night lamp, the round, dirty stone that Briar, Tris, and Daja had spelled a year before to hold light for her. Sandry was afraid of the dark. On nights like this, Briar didn't blame her in the least.

She sat next to him on the mattress, her white nightdress billowing. Her stone lamp went on the floor in front of them.

After a moment Briar whispered, "Maybe I should pick yesterday for a birthday. The day Flick—died."

"Whatever for?" asked Sandry quietly. "Birthdays are supposed to be happy days."

"But then I'd be remembering her, right? She wouldn't be dead, if I remembered her on my birthday. It wouldn't be so bad that—that I let her go."

"That isn't the way to remember her, Briar," Sandry told him gravely, sounding as kind and wise as Lark. "She wouldn't like it."

Briar shook his head. "How would you know what she'd like and what she wouldn't?"

Sandry rubbed her hand over his hair. "Because no one who's truly your friend would want you to feel bad for knowing them."

That struck home. He would need to think it over,

of course, but he had the sense that she was in the right of it.

Daja arrived next, a lit incense stick in her fingers. It gave off fragrant, rose-scented smoke as she waved it in each corner, chasing out bad air as Traders did for nightmares. Once finished, she sat crosslegged on the floor, putting the incense in a little holder beside the lamp.

Last of all came Tris, a black crocheted shawl over her nightgown. On one forefinger she carried a ruffled bird that blinked sleepily. The other three stared at the bird in wonder. The summer before they had helped Tris raise a young starling named Shriek. In the autumn, after their return from a trip to northern Emelan, Shriek had taken wing with a flock of other starlings, headed south. Since no other birds of his kind came near humans, they had to believe this was Shriek, back after months away.

Tris held the starling out to Briar. He took the bird gently as Tris sat, fussing with her nightgown and shawl until they were arranged to her satisfaction. When Briar returned her starling, Shriek trundled up her arm and into her unruly curls, where he promptly went back to sleep. Little Bear settled too, warming Briar's back. The four remained silent, thinking their own thoughts, as the night slowly wound down.

If Rosethorn had any thoughts when she entered Briar's room before dawn and found all four of her charges sleeping there, she kept them to herself. Instead she woke the boy without disturbing the others and signaled that he'd better get ready to go.

Air Temple services were held at dawn. Soon after the hymns of greeting to the sun ended, Crane and a company of young men and women in Air yellow, Water blue, or novice white came to the greenhouse door where Rosethorn and Briar waited. Briar squinted at Crane's following. Every one of them sported a large crimson dot on the forehead, to tell the world they didn't have blue pox. He was also curious. Didn't Crane say he had no help just the day before? Who were these people, then?

"Rosethorn," Crane said. He looked at Briar and sniffed, then unlocked the door. It opened into a third of the greenhouse Briar had never seen, hidden behind drapes on its glass walls. "Osprey, show the boy our clean-up procedures. Make sure he is *thorough*. Then take him around." To the Water dedicate and Rosethorn, Crane said, "It will be some time before the cleansing and robing rooms are clear. I have tea waiting in my office."

Osprey, Crane's yellow-robed apprentice, was a full-figured young woman with curly black hair. She sized Briar up through eyes a darker shade of green than his own, nodded, and jerked her head at the door. Briar followed, as did all of the other workers.

The men actually showed him the scrubbing procedure, since the women cleaned up in a separate

138

cubicle. It worked much like the bath in the tent the day before, which was almost comforting. Briar recognized medicinal herbs and oils in the rinses as well as the soaps, ones he knew well. Better still, this washroom was warmer than the tent had been. As the sun's early rays struck the high glass walls over the shrouding drapes, the whole building began to heat up.

Once they were clean, Briar and the young men donned treated caps, robes, masks, gloves, stockings that tied over the knee, and slippers. Everything in the boy's size lay under a slate with his name chalked on it. Once more he got a sense of Lark and Sandry in all that he put on. It gave him heart, as it had done in Urda's House.

"I don't envy this lad," a young man commented. "*He* has to work in the Master's private workroom."

"Don't get comfortable," advised another man, tying on his mask. "Nobody lured into his lordship's private lair has lasted a whole day. Some of us *outer* workroom slaves have endured a week or more."

They led him into a big room fitted with cabinets, braziers, counters, water kettles, and a vast tub that held steaming water by a glass wall. Once he had adjusted to the glitter of magic that lay over it all, and the heavy scent of cleansing oils and washes, Briar was fascinated. All the floors and walls were hard-glazed tile or marble except for the longest glass wall and the ceiling. When Briar knelt to inspect a drain in the

139

floor, a youth said, "Every night when we're gone, they fill both the inner and the outer workrooms with steam. It carries special chemicals and oils, to purify everything. All our cabinets are tight-fitted to keep water out, and we leave the glass and porcelain on the counters to be cleansed. It costs, but his Lordship dedicated his *personal* fortune to this greenhouse."

Osprey told Briar who everyone was, pointing to each as she gave the name. "No sense in memorizing them, though," she said, her black-fringed green eyes dancing over her mask. "Most of them will be gone in a few days."

"*Please*, gods," chorused her crew. They were laying out bottles, trays, measuring spoons, and countless other mysterious objects Briar couldn't name.

"When he ejects you from the inner workroom, come have supper with us at the Table of the Useless in the dining hall," suggested a man called Acacia. "There's what, twenty now? We had to move two tables together last night."

Briar stared at them. He felt as if he'd been magically transported to a foreign land where he spoke none of the language. One day ago he'd been trapped in a damp, gloomy house where people raved in fever dreams and those who cared for them did so in tight-lipped silence. Now he was in a room filled with light, air, and warmth, among people who joked as if the blue pox were inconvenient, as if there were life away from sickbeds and the biting scent of willowbark tea. Only when he noted the speed at which they worked, writing labels, filling bottles and jars, loading wire racks with glassware, scrubbing, mincing bundles of herbs, did he think these people knew that things were desperate at Urda's House and the other infirmaries.

At a wall beside an open doorway—to Crane's "lair," he assumed—two gloved, robed, and masked figures labored in silence. Briar moved close to watch as they drew liquid through narrow holes in sealed jars, dripping it into inch-deep wells in a thick crystal plate.

"They have the scary job," Osprey said quietly in Briar's ear. When he looked at her, she explained, "They infuse the disease in those jars. The samples we get"—she pointed to stacks of familiar-looking metal boxes near the two silent workers—"are steeped in a special liquid. It draws out the essence of the disease, then fades. Only the blue pox remains. Samples from each patient go into a row of seven wells, three such rows to a tray. *That* goes into the other workroom for his lordship to play with. Out here we all handle the disease. People tire quickly on that task, and we don't dare make any mistakes. Our robes aren't airtight. One little droplet would be deadly."

"They dish out blue pox?" whispered Briar, not sure he'd understood her properly.

"It's not the pox that kills people, you know," said Osprey, watching the pair as intently as Briar. "It's the fever that comes with it."

"I know," he replied bleakly.

Osprey glanced at him. "Wait—didn't someone tell me it was you and Dedicate Rosethorn—? At Urda's House?"

Briar nodded. Slowly he walked over until he could see the liquid as it was poured. This was the enemy that killed Flick, drooling in pale gold strings from tiny glass ladles.

"Come on," Osprey said when he moved away from the jars. "Here's the inner workroom." She motioned toward the open doorway next to the blue pox workers.

If the outer workroom was grand, the inner was enough to stagger a boy from Deadman's District, once he could see through the blaze of magic that shone everywhere. Two walls were entirely glass; two were covered with valuable procelain tiles that reached from the marble floor to the glass roof. Long counters ran down both glass walls and a third of the longer tiled wall. Every other inch of wall space, even under the counters, held watertight cabinets. Only the tall cabinets against the long tiled wall had no doors. On their shelves rested the crystal trays used for blue pox samples.

"Crane wants you working up trays." Osprey

pointed to the table at the tiled wall, between the open cabinets. A large slate hung there with a detailed list of instructions written in chalk. On the table was a stepped rack of thin bottles. Each bottle sported a paper label; seven also bore a string from which a numbered paper tag hung.

"You'll get your trays here, once the blue pox is added." She went to the open cabinet at their right, between the table and the doorway to the outer workroom. "Always keep the trays level"—very carefully she lifted one from the shelf—"because if you tilt them, blue pox will drip out. That is bad."

"Lakik, yes!" whispered Briar.

"If any gets into the other wells on the tray, the whole thing's ruined. If you leak or drip, whatever happens, don't make a fuss. Bring it *quietly* to the washers at the tub. If Crane finds out you slipped, you're out."

"A dreadful fate, to be sure," muttered Briar, startling a chuckle from her. Made bold by that, he added, "I don't see how you can work with that Bag. You seem all right, but he's such a pickle-faced cull from an overbred litter—"

"I don't know how you work with Rosethorn without bleeding to death," she said frankly. "She's that sharp with everyone." Her eyes met Briar's over their masks; both of them smiled. "To each his—or her—own, I suppose," Osprey admitted. "Now. Trays. Put

143

the glass lid aside, gently. *Very* gently. Follow the instructions on the board, there."

Briar read them carefully:

To Well numbered 1 Add 2 drops liquid from Bottle numbered 1.
To Well numbered 2 Add 1 drop liquid from Bottle numbered 2.
To Well numbered 3 Add 1 measure powder from Bottle
    numbered 3.
To Well numbered 4 Add 3 drops liquid from Bottle numbered 4.
To Well numbered 5 Add 2 drops liquid from Bottle numbered 5.
To Well numbered 6 Add 1 drop liquid from Bottle numbered 6.
To Well numbered 7 Add 1 drop liquid from Bottle numbered 7.

Glancing at the tray as Osprey drew liquids or powders from the numbered bottles and slid them into the wells, he saw that a number was cut into the stone beside each well. There were seven in a row, which meant they tried seven possible cures on the pox liquid from three different people, all on one tray.

"I can do this," he remarked, surprised.

"All you need is the ability to pay attention and steady hands," Osprey remarked. "Once you're done . . ." She eased the glass lid onto the tray and secured it. Then she put the tray on a shelf in the cabinet to their left. "You can't let your mind wander. Once things get started, Crane and whoever is helping him will change the instructions on your board," she explained. "I'll help you get any new supplies and change the number tags, at least until you get the

144

hang of things. You're smart, or Rosenthorn never would have borne with you for a whole year. She—uh-oh." Osprey had seen something in the outer workroom that she didn't like. Briar followed her as she hurried through the doorway.

"Yellowrose, careful!" she told one of the pair handling the blue pox essence. "Your sleeve, your left sleeve—"

The youth about to dip his measure into the jar froze. The string that gathered his sleeve at one wrist had come undone. The sleeve had escaped the cuff on his glove to hang perilously close to the tray he was filling.

Crane, Rosethorn, and the Water dedicate had come in, washed and robed. "You." Crane pointed to Yellowrose, his hand drooping from a rigid, accusing forefinger. "Yellowrose. Out."

"I didn't get it in—" protested the youth.

"Out," Crane repeated icily. "Now."

Yellowrose put down his measure and did as he was told. As he walked to the washroom, Briar saw a number of gloved hands pat the reject in comfort.

Crane went to the glass wall behind the large boiling vat, wiped away the steam, and rapped on the glass. A face pressed against it on the outside: a temple runner.

"Two more helpers," Crane said loudly. "Two, understand?"

"Two?" a girl murmured.

"In case someone else errs," said Crane. He turned to inspect the room, his weary brown eyes missing nothing. He pointed out things for each worker to correct, then entered the inner workroom.

"Come on," Rosethorn murmured to Briar. "Time to get your feet wet."

9

Rosethorn strode to the counter at the far side of Crane's room, placing a satchel on it. She began to empty the bag, placing its contents—her own blends of oils, infusions, and herbs—in neat ranks against the glass wall. The Water dedicate, who someone had greeted as Peachleaf, dragged a tall clerk's chair to the end of Crane's worktable and began to take pens, paper, and ink from the cabinet underneath. Crane himself arranged things on the counter at his end: vials, lenses of all kinds and colors, sheets of paper, and a priceless Yanjing porcelain teacup tinted celestial blue. Briar's fingers itched, not just because that cup was worth a fortune. It was one of the most beautiful things he'd ever seen.

Crane walked over to Briar's station. "If it goes missing, I will know where to look," he said ominously. "You are here to *work*." Raising his voice so it would carry, he told Rosethorn, "I will treat him as I would any other novice. If he cannot be relied upon, he goes. I cannot do my own work and watch his too. He really is too young for this."

Rosethorn's only reply was an absentminded, "Where are the notes to date?"

"Peachleaf?" asked Crane drily. "Did you make a second copy as I requested?"

The Water dedicate looked around frantically, then rummaged in the cabinet where she kept her supplies. Crane went over to complain and to supervise.

Waiting for him, Briar read the instructions on the slate with care. He then picked up the numbered vials and matched them to the wells with the same number on the tray before him.

You'd have a real mess if you jumbled the notes for it all, he thought. No wonder Crane gets testy. Not, added Briar with a grim eye on the man, that I mean to be lambkin-meek if he gets testy with *me*. In a box next to the rack of additives he found measuring tools, pens, ink, and squares of parchment for labels. A note was stuck to the inside of the lid, with the instructions: *Give everything to washers at end of day!*

"Finally!" Crane announced as Peachleaf held up a sheaf of papers. He passed them to Rosethorn and came back to Briar. "Attend," he began.

"Osprey showed me. I just follow the slate," Briar said, cutting off the lecture before Crane could give it. He got to work, adding liquids and powders in the proper wells as he kept hands and arms clear of the tray itself. Though he'd never had to do this particular job before, Rosenthorn's demands for her medicines and herbal mixtures were every bit as precise as Crane's. Briar moved from bottle or jar to tray steadily, barely hearing Crane's fusses about being careful and watching where his fingers went. Once he finished the entire tray, he opened an inkwell, took a reed pen, and carefully noted the date on parchment labels glued to the edge of the tray.

"Well?" he said, looking up.

Crane's eyebrows went down. Briar figured the dedicate was scowling under his mask. At last Crane pointed to a final note on the slate: *Variation L.* Briar wrote that under the date on the labels.

"Cover it," Crane said tartly, "then shelve it."

Briar slid the tray into a space on the left-hand shelves. He grinned evilly at Crane, who couldn't see beneath the boy's mask. "I learnt steadiness picking locks in Baghouses," Briar said airily.

Someone—he suspected it was Peachleaf—snickered. Crane only raised an eyebrow at him and said, "Next tray."

He stood over Briar for three more trays, watching every step. When Osprey brought supplies from the outer workroom, Crane made Briar refill his bottles and jars, then slip the numbered labels back on. Finally he went to his own table and got to work.

Off and on Briar would peer at him, amazed at the variety of the magics Crane used. The man treated the contents of the trays with his own liquids and powders, each of them so powerful that their containers shone like miniature suns when Briar looked at them for very long. He could see magic glint on the surface of the many different lenses that Crane used to examine the trays. Even the air around Crane was filled with traces and sprinkles of silvery magic that flared whenever he spoke a fresh spell.

At midmorning Briar placed a finished tray on the shelf. Feeling he'd earned a short halt, the boy stretched and looked around. Peachleaf sorted through a sheaf of parchments, her hands trembling. Rosethorn continued to read Crane's notes with the kind of concentration she normally kept for mildews and plant lice. In the outer workroom Briar could hear the soft murmur of conversation over the clink of glass and metal.

Crane drifted to Briar's post, frowning over a sheaf of notes. When Briar turned back to his counter, Crane held up a hand, meaning for him to wait. The lanky dedicate mixed three oils from Briar's supplies into a new bottle. The boy frowned. He could see that

Crane had used marshmallow and holly oils, but he couldn't identify the third ingredient. Reaching into the new bottle with his power, he choked.

"Mustard?" he asked, shocked. "What good will that do?"

"Are you a healer as well as a plant mage?" was the acid reply. Crane briskly tied the Number Four label to the new oil's bottle. "You haven't the training to understand, nor have I time to instruct you."

Be that way, Briar thought irritably. As Crane changed the slate to read one drop instead of three for Number Four, Briar took out a clean measure. He noticed that Crane had also changed the letter of variation on the blackboard.

"I have amended—" Crane began.

"I see," Briar interrupted, too peeved to mind his manners. "Variation M." *What'll we do when we run out of letters?* he wondered.

As the boy fetched a new tray, Crane said grudgingly, "It is my thought that essence of mustard will act to flush the disease, as the marshmallow soothes the harsh action of the mustard. The holly—"

"Fever," Briar said promptly.

"It won't work," called Rosethorn. Crane twitched. Rosethorn went on, "Check your notes on the combinations you tried two days ago."

Crane went over to her, and Briar tended his tray. The sound of rising voices broke his concentration soon afterward: Crane and Rosethorn were fighting.

Peachleaf, seated too close to them for her own comfort, shrank back, face pale. Briar, noting the healthy blush in Rosethorn's cheeks, decided she was having a good time and ignored the battle. He had completed half of the waiting trays about an hour before noon, but someone from the outer room carried in fresh ones.

"Use the old trays first," Crane said. Briar nodded. He hated to admit it and would never say it aloud, but Crane seemed to have good reasons to do things as he did.

He was measuring out infused aloe from jar Number Seven when Rosethorn asked, "Crane, why did we create broad diagnosis powders three years ago if you aren't going to use them?"

"What are you talking about?" demanded Crane. "Of course I used them on the day we began. I had to give them up—it is in your very first section of notes."

"No, it's not."

Crane went to Rosethorn's table and plucked the notes from her fingers. "I detailed the results thoroughly," he muttered, leafing through the sheets. "The blue pox caused our general diagnosis additives to break up. I know very well you are to have *everything* . . . Ah." With a glare for Peachleaf, he pulled three sheets from the stack and put them on top. The healer shrank in her chair. "They *appear* to have been placed behind the section on the disease's response to neutral substances. Why, no one can know, because

152

these notes are supposed to be in chronological order." He thrust the papers at Rosethorn.

She took them and muttered, "Bully."

Crane ignored her. "Even the most basic compound additives we are accustomed to using break up when brought into contact with the blue pox essence. I was forced to go to the simplest oils, chemicals, and herbs. It slowed me to a crawl."

Rosethorn frowned as she read. "That makes no sense," she remarked.

Crane saw that Briar was watching. His eyebrows rose, and Briar quickly got back to his work.

When the Hub clock chimed the half hour after noon, Osprey and another of the outer-room workers arrived with a tray of covered dishes. Once her companion had set up a small table at the empty center of the room, Osprey began to lay out the dishes and eating utensils she carried. Briar, who had just finished a tray, went to help.

"Take off the gloves and mask—I'll give you a fresh set when you're ready to start again," Osprey murmured to Briar. "Don't go near the worktables while you're eating. You just cost Ibis and Nomi a copper astrel apiece. They were sure you wouldn't last till noon. Fill yourself a plate and eat—you need it to stay fresh."

Briar was happy to do as he was bid. He also filled a plate for Rosethorn. "You betting?" he asked, his voice audible only to Osprey.

She grinned at him. Briar liked her grin; it was wide and cheerful and sunny. "I have three copper crescents on you getting the gate between two and three. He hates interrupting to eat, even though he knows he must, so he's testy for hours after."

"Put me down for two copper creses around four," Briar replied, straight-faced. "I'll be tired of his fussing by then."

"Can't do it," Osprey said. "The one that's bet on can't wager on himself."

"All right." Briar glanced at Peachleaf, who scribbled madly, trying to keep up with the murmured instructions Crane gave as he worked. "Two copper creses on Peachleaf by three. He keeps having to spell words for her when he's giving her notes."

"Two creses on Peachleaf at three. Right." Osprey and her companion left.

Lunch reassured Briar a little. It gave him the crawls to think of the blue pox all around him, but the food was very good. Maybe even working for Crane was better than quarantine.

He made sure that Rosethorn ate. She had finished reading Crane's notes and had arranged her counter the way she liked. Many of the articles—lenses, glass bottles, herbal pastes, a set of crystals—were things he'd never seen before. Briar had been so positive he'd inspected all she had, over the winter. If he'd missed these items, she was trickier than he'd ever suspected.

Briar returned to his desk, glad for the time away,

and found that more trays had been added to the stack of those awaiting his attentions.

After his return, he saw that Crane was looking over his shoulder again. Several times Briar nearly told the man that if he'd wanted to be minded by a fidget, he'd have stayed at Urda's House. Thinking about Ibis's and Nomi's bets, he held his tongue. He'd hate to make money for anyone who'd bet on his departure that day.

Perhaps it was relief, once Crane returned to his own labors. Perhaps it was the break for lunch. He might simply have adjusted to all the magic in his surroundings. Whatever the cause, soon after Crane's retreat Briar saw a wink of silver in the wells on the tray in his hands.

Don't get excited, he ordered himself, closing his eyes to rest them. It's reflected magic or something. There's glass enough here to blind a kid with reflections. He opened his eyes. If he'd seen magic in this tray, it was gone. Shaking his head, he added oils and powders, wrote out labels, clipped the lid to the tray, and then shelved it. When he went for the next tray, he stopped before the cabinet where they were stacked, his back to the glass walls, and took the lid from the topmost one. Gently he lowered the tray into his body's shadow and looked down into it. A ghost of silver glided across the liquid in the third well; hints of it shone in several more. They faded. Briar whistled and carried the tray to his worktable.

155

Was he seeing *magic* in the blue pox?

"Asaia Bird-Winged, give me patience and give me strength," announced Crane. "How often must I spell so common a term as 'antipyretic'?"

"Couldn't I just write 'fever reducer'? squeaked Peachleaf.

"Whatever term will stop your inane questions," Crane told her icily as the Hub clock chimed two. "Read back that last sentence."

As Peachleaf read, Briar added oil from the Number One bottle to the three Number One wells on his tray. His two copper crescents on Peachleaf's three o'clock dismissal were safe for now.

When he fetched the next tray, he again put his body between it and the light sources. He *thought* he may have seen a glimmer, but it was gone on second look. What he needed was Niko, or more likely, Tris. Niko was busy in the city. While Briar, Daja, and Sandry had caught the ability to see magic from Tris, back when their powers were seeping into each other, Tris was still the best at it. She claimed it was because Niko had bespelled her eyeglasses to help her to see power. Briar suspected that Niko had just taken the easy way to teach her the skill.

Whatever the reason, Briar was sure that if magic were part of the blue pox, Tris would see it. But how was she to get the chance? People did not come and go in these workrooms. Anyone who entered had business here, and they had to scrub coming and going. He couldn't just ask Tris to ramble by and peer in.

Glass shattered noisily in the outer workroom. Immediately Osprey shouted, "Don't worry, it's not the pox—just some clean glassware. Not a problem!"

Crane floated through the door like a god of swans, red flags of rage riding high on his sallow cheeks. Stiff-necked old piece of codfish bait, thought Briar, carrying his newest tray to his counter.

"You, and you." Crane's voice was almost gentle. "Out. Tell them to send more workers, and quickly."

"Write the words you have trouble with on a scrap of paper and keep it nearby," Rosethorn whispered to Peachleaf.

"I do," sniffed the Water dedicate, "but they fall off the table!"

"Put them where your sleeves won't knock them off," Rosethorn hissed. "Honestly, Peachleaf, you're the best midwife at Winding Circle—try to be more confident. Stand up to him."

Briar shook his head, writing his labels neatly. Some people might stand up to Crane, he guessed, but Peachleaf wasn't one of them.

Collecting a new tray, Briar checked it as he had the other two. This time he was almost certain magic was there. He might fare better if he looked into the jars where the essence of the disease was brewed, but the thought of doing so made his scalp creep. He wasn't sick yet—he'd checked his reflection in the glass wall after lunch—and he planned not to be, ever.

Crane returned. Briar had the chance to work up three trays before he heard Crane say, "That—is—it."

Briar looked around. Peachleaf had spilled a bottle of ink.

The lordly forefinger pointed. "Out," Crane ordered.

Peachleaf sighed. "*Thank* you," she said, gripping the pointing hand and giving it two hearty shakes. "I won't take a moment more of your time. Come see me if you ever want a baby delivered." She trotted out of the room with a wave to Briar.

The Hub clock chimed the half hour. Drat, thought the boy glumly. I lost the bet. He risked a peek at Crane.

The man surveyed Peachleaf's notes. "Now what am I to do?" he demanded, forgetting perhaps that he was not alone. "Today has been virtually a complete waste."

Rosethorn faced him, leaning against her counter. "You could always take your own notes," she said mockingly.

Crane sighed. "Have you forgotten I need my hands free to work?"

"You just like having someone to order around." Crane glared at Rosethorn. When he didn't speak she continued, "Why not Osprey? She's sharp enough, *and* she puts up with you."

"I require her where she is," replied Crane, sagging against his own counter. "I can trust her to watch those flibbertigibbets out there and make sure they do nothing to kill us all. I told you, I will not risk those who show an aptitude for this in a mad scramble for a cure. She must learn to take each step carefully before moving on to the next—such lessons are impossible under these conditions."

"You may have to make allowances," Rosethorn pointed out. "You may have to take a risk."

"I have put five years' training into Osprey alone—" Crane began.

Briar croaked, "Tris."

Crane's head swiveled in his direction. "I beg your pardon?" he asked coolly.

Rosethorn silently adjusted the strings of her mask.

"My—my mate, Tris," Briar said. "The redhead."

"You are too young to have a mate," drawled Crane.

"It's street slang for best friend," Rosethorn explained scornfully. "As you'd know if you ever dropped out of your alabaster tower and dealt with real people in real places."

Crane sighed. "Had I wished to do so, I never would have taken vows." He turned back to Briar. "Recording notes is more demanding than preparing trays."

"She reads and writes good," returned Briar,

thickening his street accent out of perversity. "*And she remembers the first time you tell her how a thing's spelt, because she hates bein' ignorant. She reads books, thick ones, all the time."

"She also has nothing to do," added Rosethorn thoughtfully, "and she hates that."

Briar stared at her, amazed. He'd never thought Rosethorn had noticed.

"She is a *child*," Crane replied stiffly, turning away.

Silence fell once more as Rosethorn got back to work. Crane muttered to himself as he tried both to do his spells and to write out what he'd done. Briar shut his ears to the distraction. Half an hour passed before Crane went to the doorway. "Osprey."

Osprey walked over. "Sir?"

"Tell the runners I want the girl Trisana from Discipline called over here—"

"Tsk, tsk," Rosethorn said mockingly from her station. "I can't imagine *you* would have forgotten that our four charges speak mind-to-mind without physical contact."

"I think the tea's boiling over," muttered Osprey, darting away.

"Rosethorn," Crane said ominously.

Tris? Briar mind-called. *Would you come to the greenhouse? We've something for you to do—taking notes for Old Picklepuss Crane.*

Finally! was her elated reponse. *Just let me tell Lark! Thank you!*

160

Don't thank me, Briar thought. *Crane rides folk hard.*

I don't care if he rides me with a bit and spurs. At least I'll be doing something! Now, how do I get in there?

He explained about the washroom, then let her go. He had thought to mention his suspicions, but in the end he chose to keep quiet. If there was magic to be seen, Tris would notice without prompting. If he mentioned it beforehand, it might plant the idea in her head, making her see its flicker if it was there or not.

It was half an hour before Osprey came to the workroom door. "Sir, the girl Trisana from Discipline is here." Tris walked in, robed, masked, gloved, capped, and shod as they all were. Her wiry hair fought the cap, forcing red curls out from under the cloth. In one hand she carried her wooden writing-case.

Crane gestured to it. "You should not have fetched that. We have writing materials enough, and you won't be able to take it out of here until we have a cure for the disease—if we find one."

Tris looked at her case, then shrugged. "I still would have brought this," she told Crane. "Everything's how I like it." She squared her shoulders. "Where do I sit?"

Crane pointed to Peachleaf's chair and even managed to wait until Tris was settled before he began to explain how he wanted things done. Briar returned to work, trying not to feel restless. Had she seen it? Or had the other magics in these rooms blinded her to any ghostly shimmer in the trays?

There was no more time to think. First Rosethorn, then Crane made changes to the additives for the trays. Putting old blends away and making up new ones kept Briar occupied for some time. Once that was done, he started a new tray.

"I asked, could you wait a moment, please?" That was Tris, ominously patient.

"My dear young woman, if you cannot keep up with me—" Crane began.

"You just gave me a list of numbers, Dedicate. Which would you prefer, that I get them down as you gave them to me, or that I hurry and make mistakes?"

Briar waited, but Crane did not reply. Risking a glance, Briar saw that Crane drummed his worktable with his fingers as he glared at Tris. The girl wrote something carefully, then said, "All right."

Crane resumed his dictation. Briar worked on as tension ebbed from the air. That's one, he thought, dripping mullein oil into three wells. Just let her keep him happy till she sees the magic in the pox, that's all I ask. He wasn't sure who he asked it of. Lakik the Trickster was a bad god to ask for anything but ill luck to enemies, and Onini had no interest in medicine things. Urda, perhaps. She was the goddess with a stake in all this.

162

Crane and Rosethorn continued to change the ingredients Briar used, marking some trays to be kept overnight, telling him to get rid of others. That job alone was scary: the trays had to be carried into the outer workroom to be emptied and boiled. He did *not* want to spill anything.

The clock struck, though Briar wasn't sure of the hour, just before he heard Tris say, "Just a moment— you said three drops of *elecampane* essence?"

"Rather clearly, as I recall," Crane replied.

"But you added three drops not so long ago."

"I did not."

"Yes, you did, around two o'clock," replied Tris. She flipped through a sheaf of notes. "Right here. See?"

Crane looked over Tris's shoulder. "Those are not your notes."

"They're your last scribe's. I looked through while you were getting supplies."

"You just happened to remember." Briar couldn't tell if Crane was sarcastic or thoughtful.

"I *remembered*," drawled Tris, much like Crane, "because I memorized the spelling of elecampane, in case you needed it again."

Crane looked up and saw that not only was Briar watching, but Rosethorn as well. "Do I afford you amusement?" he wanted to know.

"Yes," Rosethorn told him immediately.

Briar ducked his head and acted busy.

There had been no fresh changes to his slate for over an hour when he stopped for a stretch. Looking up, he was startled to find the sky overhead was turning dark. Rosethorn had chosen this moment to rest too: she watched Crane and Tris as she leaned against her table.

As if Crane felt the change in the air, he straightened and braced his hands against the small of his back, twisting to loosen it. "Put your brush down," he advised Tris. "Move a little."

Tris slid off the chair, making a face when her stiff legs hit the floor. Slowly she walked over to examine Briar's work area. He waited until she squinted at the tray he was about to start, then said quietly, "That yellow stuff, that's the blue pox. They render it in there—" He pointed to the outer workroom. "Then they put it in these rock trays, and I drip things in each pocket with the blue pox."

Tris frowned. Silently she asked, *What did you put in this tray?* She looked at the racks of containers from which Briar made his additions to the pox essence. *None of this is magicked, but I keep glimpsing it.*

Briar felt the back of his neck tingle. Did she see it! *There's only blue pox in that tray. I ain't done nothing to it yet.*

Tris gripped Briar's arm. *Just the disease? Are the trays magicked?*

Briar shook his head.

Can I see the blue pox? she asked. *Just the blue pox?*

Briar led Tris into the outer workroom. Osprey was lifting crystal trays from the boiling vat and setting them to dry. "Tris, here's Osprey—she's Crane's apprentice."

Osprey nodded cheerfully at Tris. "He must like you. I haven't heard him deliver a lordly denunciation yet."

Tris shrugged. "He'll get to it soon enough."

"I wanted to show Tris the blue pox," explained Briar. "She ought to see how it's brewed up, since she's to be a scholar one day."

Osprey shed the special mitts that led her handle the hot crystal slabs without burning herself and donned treated gloves again. As she led Tris to the counter where workers handled the blue pox essence, she explained how it was made.

As carefully as if she handled feather-thin glass, Osprey opened the metal catches that locked a jar and raised the lid. Tris leaned close to look; Briar did the same. Inside the jar was glazed white. It was half full of the yellowish, oily-looking blue pox essence.

Briar saw an assortment of silver glints, a shimmer that faded. Slipping through their magical connection, he gazed at the essence through Tris's eyes. To her the silver was no rapidly fading glimpse, but a steady, pale gleam.

"The stuff used to make the essence, it's magicked, isn't it?" Tris asked Osprey.

"Well, yes," replied the young woman, "but the clarifying wash—that's what it's called—the wash is made to evaporate once the disease is pulled from the samples. There can't be any magic left in the essence. If it is, all our results will be wrong. The cures won't work, or they'll go *really* awry. May I close the jar?"

"I did not mean for you go on holiday," announced Crane meaningfully from the inner workroom.

"One moment," Tris said to Osprey. She leaned over the jar, squinting at its contents. Briar, looking again through her eyes, saw the wash of silver.

This is why you suggested me, isn't it? demanded Tris. *You weren't sure, and you thought if you told me what you thought you saw, you might make me see it.*

That's about right, Briar acknowledged, and braced himself for her wrath.

Smart thinking, she told him instead.

Briar drew out of her magic, startled. He could have sworn she'd be vexed.

Tris returned to Crane without a word to Osprey. "She gets distracted," Briar said apologetically to the apprentice. "Thanks for showing it to her."

"It's all right," Osprey assured Briar. "Working for Crane, you get used to people who forget the niceties when they're caught up."

Briar snorted. "I guess you would." He followed Tris.

"If we are ready?" Crane asked Tris. "Now that playtime is over?"

Tris took a deep breath. "You should send for Niko. There's magic in the pox."

Crane stared at her, unmoving. Fascinated, Briar counted as the man blinked—once. Twice. Three times.

He heard a click as Rosethorn put something down on her own counter, hard. "You see magic?" she asked sharply. "Are you sure?"

Tris nodded.

"We have substances that tell us if magic is in use," Crane pointed out. "We employed those first."

"Does it work if it's only a sneeze-worth of magic?" Briar wanted to know. "I mean, it was so teeny I wasn't even sure I saw it."

"And thus you suggested Niklaren Goldeye's student," Crane said.

"I don't know what kind of measure a sneeze-worth is," Tris remarked. "But the amount is *very* small."

Rosethorn came over. "Do you think it's possible?" she asked Crane. "That it could be missed?"

"Or it may have been lost among all our other magics," he admitted. "We cannot do any of this without a monumental use of power, but—there are drawbacks. We could have overlooked an infinitesimal amount of magic. Osprey!" He raised his voice so abruptly that Tris, Briar, and Rosethorn were all caught by surprise and jumped.

Osprey came in at a run. "Sir?" she gasped.

"We require Niklaren Goldeye. Wherever he is, here or in Summersea, find him *at once.*"

10

Niko was in the city. Messengers rode there to find him while the workroom was closed for its nightly cleaning. Briar, Tris, and Rosethorn returned to Discipline.

Crane came too. He and Rosethorn were involved in a long debate, trying to create a new course of action. They had talked as they scrubbed, shouting to be heard in the washroom. They'd continued all the way to Discipline, squinting in moonlight to read their notes, and debated while nearly everyone else had supper and went to bed.

The dawn bell woke the sleepers. As they emerged

from their rooms, they discovered that Niko had come. He sat with Crane and Rosethorn, who appeared not to have gone to bed at all.

"Tris," Niko said, "eat breakfast quickly, please. We're riding to Summersea."

"One moment." Crane looked as if he'd been caught by surprise. "Why her? Her vision-skills aren't as strong as yours—"

"Thanks ever so," Tris mumbled, pouring tea for herself.

"I can make far better use of her," persisted Crane. "There is work to do as we await your results."

"You cannot make better use of her," Niko said sharply, dark eyes glittering. "I will have to do a past-visualization working at some point. For it I require her strength and stubbornness. An extra pair of eyes will not come amiss, nor her ability to control water."

"She is a clear and accurate note-taker," protested Crane. "She thinks about the notes she is given. I made infinitely more progress yesterday, with her and Rosethorn and the boy, than I had until then."

Rosethorn flapped a hand as if she fanned herself. "Spare my blushes," she murmured. Briar snorted.

"I do not begrudge the acknowledgment of credit where it is due," replied Crane loftily. "We have a good team. Breaking it up now is most ill-advised."

"Find another scribe," Niko snapped. "I'll have the duke send his, if necessary—"

"Is this what it'll be like when I'm older and boys are fighting for the chance to kiss my hand?" Tris murmured to Sandry. The noble giggled.

"I do not want a ducal scribe; I want this girl. May I remind you—"

"I will not go into the sewers without her!" Niko barked.

Everyone stared at him. Tris turned white. "Sewers?" she squeaked.

"The disease spreads as the water level in the sewers rises and damaged pipes leak into wells. It's plain the two are connected," Niko said. "If we are to go there without drowning, I need Tris. If I am to have power to work the spells that reveal the past and to follow the trail to whatever mage concocted this— horror—I will need Tris. No one else will do."

"Not the sewers," whispered the redhead, trembling. "They're *dirty*."

"I know," replied Niko, his voice sharp.

For a long moment, no one said a word. Finally Crane sighed. "May she return to me when you are done?"

"I don't *want* to go," complained Tris. "Can't I stay with Crane and Rosethorn?"

"We must," Niko retorted. "Eat your breakfast."

"I'm not hungry."

"Then change into old clothes. We need to do this *now*."

Tris walked to the stair, her feet dragging. Sandry

followed her friend upstairs. "It'll be all right," those seated below heard her say.

"I hope so," murmured Niko, rubbing his temples.

Just after Tris and Niko left, Frostpine arrived at Discipline. "More work for us," he told Daja as she ate breakfast. "Protective talismans for the duke's soldiers, to keep a rain of chamber pots and rocks from banging them on the head in the East District. I'd hoped they'd forgotten I can do such things, but someone apparently remembered."

Crane raised her eyebrows. "How can you object to the protection of those who keep the duke's peace?"

Frostpine sat next to Daja, plucking morsels from a muffin and popping them into his mouth. "A proper fear of such things keeps soldiers polite," he observed. "Otherwise they might be tempted to push common folk around. Orders to enter people's homes uninvited are a sore temptation for peacekeepers, I've found."

"Have you any respect for proper order?" asked Crane.

"Depends on whose idea of order it is," said Frostpine. "Daja, are you about done?"

She nodded, eating quickly.

Crane shook his head. "Rosethorn? Briar? We should go."

As the others left, Sandry lay her head on the table. She was one solid ache, head to toe. A cool

172

hand rested on her forehead; blearily she looked up at Lark. "I'm just tired," she said. "I'm not sick."

"We're both tired," replied Lark. "I really hate to do this, but—we've been at it for days. I think we have to rest. No work, just rest."

"But Crane needs masks and gloves—" argued Sandry. The idea of a day without pouring her magic into a slush of herbs, oils, and powders made her giddy.

"He's got enough for two days," Lark said firmly. "We really must stop for a while. Go back to bed, dear one. I'm doing the same—the dishes can wait until we get up."

Crane, Rosethorn, and Briar had just reached the spiral road when Rosethorn halted, staring at the north gate. A covered wagon like that which had taken her, Flick, and Briar to Urda's House rolled through. It was driven by a masked and gloved soldier of the Duke's Guard: the red spot that meant she was free of the blue pox was vivid on her forehead. When the wagon drew near, Rosethorn motioned for the driver to stop.

"Are the city hospitals full, that you bring the sick here?" she asked.

The driver shook her head. "They're near full, but the duke's putting up two more, one on Market Square and one on Fuller's Circle. These are temple folk with the blue pox—they're to be nursed here, Honored Moonstream's orders."

"Temple folk?" cried Rosethorn.

"Who?" demanded Crane, grabbing the bridle of the horse closest to him. "Do you know the names?"

"Novices Fara, Olatji, Kazem, Alasha, Nanjo," the driver recited tiredly. "Dedicates Egret, Treefrog, Henna, Whitelake. If I may—?"

Crane released the horses, and the wagon rolled on. Rosethorn was shaken and pale. Briar felt as if he'd been dropped down a hole. "Henna was fine when she left to look after the Arsenal setup," he whispered. "Just fine."

Rosethorn drew the gods-circle on her chest and closed her eyes to pray. Crane did the same. Briar waited them out as patiently as he could manage. If you give your life to a temple, he supposed, you believed that prayer worked. He knew better.

"Can we get to it?" he asked when they looked up again. "You said there's things we can do without knowing just how this magic turned into the blue pox?"

"He's right," said Rosethorn grimly. "Let's get to it. That's the only way we can help them now."

"Careful," said Niko. "One more—you're almost down."

"And oh, how pleased I am to hear that," muttered Tris.

"Can we get *on* with it?" Niko demanded. Tris was feeling for the next rung of the ladder with one foot. Like him, she wore thigh-high boots, oilcloth breeches and robe, an oilcloth cap, mask, and gloves. Like the other workers in Crane's greenhouse, she also sported a large red dot at the middle of her forehead as a sign she was uninfected with the blue pox. Niko's red dot, she'd noticed, was on the back of one hand. He never would have consented to an unsightly red mark anywhere on his face.

They had entered the system near Flick's den, taking the path that Alleypup had used to bring Rosethorn down. Niko had chosen to start where the first case of blue pox had appeared, hoping to trace its path back to its origin.

This time, when Tris put down a foot, there was a small splash and the feel of a hard, flat surface. Wincing, she put her other foot down. Another splat. She released the ladder and turned to scowl at Niko.

Light bloomed around him to reveal a ledge four feet across, spotted with dark puddles. The canal's waters ran one inch below the ledge. Tris saw lumps carried along by the swift-moving tide and rats that ran squeaking down the ledges, and cringed. The stench flooded through her nose, making her stomach roll. Trembling, she breathed with her mouth open, trying to smell only the oils in the treated cloth of her mask.

"This way, Rosethorn said." Niko towed her along until they reached Flick's den. Scavengers had been there already, taking the lamps and whatever else looked to be useful or interesting. Even the bed of rags had been picked over.

Niko removed a glove to rummage in a sack he carried on one shoulder. He produced a small stone jar and opened it. "Take off your spectacles," he ordered Tris. "Remember the vision-enhancing ointment we made earlier this year?"

"Gum mastic, cinnamon bark *and* oil, at a silver crescent the ounce, no less!—"

Niko sighed impatiently.

Tris glared at him and continued, "Heliotrope, saffron and cloves, lavender."

"Very good," Niko said. "Close your eyes."

She felt something cool dotted first on one eyelid, then the other. "Wouldn't it be better put on my specs, the same as your other vision spell?"

Niko sniffed. "That spell wore off a week after I placed it on you."

Tris donned her spectacles. "You never told me."

"It slipped my mind," he replied as he put the balm on his own eyelids, then closed the jar. "There's an advantage to instructing young mages: a suggestion counts for so much with you four. Now, what do you see?"

Her eyelids tingled. A gold veil dropped over her sight, one that shimmered and caught on objects, then pulled free. It stuck only in a wash through the sewer and on a line of footprints that turned into Flick's den.

"There's a gold tint in the water," she said, watching it. "It comes from upstream. And it's in footprints too."

"The tint is throughout the city's water. It is the footprints we must follow." Niko walked down the trail. Tris resettled her spectacles on her masked nose—they didn't fit properly with cloth in the way—and set out after him.

At first they walked in silence, intent on the trail. For some time the prints showed clear through even a slight amount of water. By the time Tris realized that either the ledge was sloping or the water was rising, she was ankle deep. "Oh, no!" she cried. "Niko, stop!"

"What's the matter?" he demanded.

"We're *walking* in it, and it's getting deeper! You don't need me for this—please let me go home! *Please!*"

Niko faced her.

"You see better than I do, and this is *disgusting*." Tris knew she was whining and was ashamed, but the horror of soggy lumps that struck her legs in the dark made her dizzy. Never in her life had she wanted to be gone from a place so badly as now.

"Stop acting like a child!" Niko snapped. "This job needs both of us, I explained that to you! Complaining about how dreadful it is only makes things worse, and I don't *need* them to be worse. I didn't ask you to come here lightly, and I would really, really appreciate it if you could just *hold your tongue*." He caught his breath and stood still for a moment, eyes closed. After a moment he said, "I hate this too, understand?"

Tris stared at him. Niko was sweating. It was damp and cold here, but she saw drops collect on his forehead. When she tentatively rested a hand on his arm, she could feel him trembling. She had been so busy worrying about herself that she had forgotten how finicky he was. He tended his clothing with minute zeal, inspected tableware in strange eating-shops for dirt that might have escaped a lazy washing, and aired out his bedding the moment he reached a new inn.

She looked at the water rolling down the tunnel toward them and thrust it aside with her power to bare the ledge. Holding it off their right, Tris said quietly, "See, everything's fine. You should have reminded me to get the water out of the way, I'd have done it. Now we can see the footprints better." She patted her teacher. "We're all right. Come on."

Wishing they had slept more, Briar followed Crane and Rosethorn into the big workroom. "If I may have your attention," Crane said.

Everyone put down their work and looked at him.

"There is a magical element to the blue pox," he announced.

Someone gasped. Two workers murmured to each other.

"May I have silence?" Crane asked, a bit too

patient. He got it instantly. "Its components have yet to be determined. We hope to know by day's end what precisely we are dealing with. Should that be the case, I believe we shall begin to make progress."

The workers nodded their agreement. Stick with Crane long enough, Briar thought, and you forget that all of these folk must be pretty smart to get sent here, with so much at stake. He treats 'em like silly bleaters, but they aren't.

"In the meantime, we must start again, with those procedures used when we know that magic is present. Additives must be prepared—Osprey knows which of the lists to use. Rosethorn and I should review the trays that were experimented upon yesterday. Then, unless we, er, got lucky—"

A soft chuckle greeted Crane's words. He pronounces it like he never said "got lucky" in his life, but he's trying to sound like one of us, Briar thought, amused. If he ain't careful, he'll break a tooth that way.

The dedicate cleared his throat. "Then, unless we stumble on something useful purely by accident, those trays must be emptied and cleaned thoroughly and quickly." Crane shrugged. "I regret to say that since we proceeded quite well yesterday, there are a great many trays to be cleaned."

A few workers groaned.

Rosethorn raised a hand for quiet. "I know this looks like a setback," she said. "The truth is, it's the

179

best news we've had in a while. At last we know *something*. All of us have worked with magic enough to know that it jumps funny sometimes, but we also know ways to detect what magic has shaped and unravel the spell. No long faces or complaints—we've finally got a direction we can follow."

"Enough loitering," said Crane. "To work, all of you." To Rosethorn he added, "I will join you in a moment. I need to look around."

Rosethorn nodded and headed for the inner workroom at her usual brisk stride. A man lifting a tray with blue pox essence turned from his counter just as Rosethorn passed and clipped her with the heavy tray. It tilted and began to slide from his grip. Instinctively Rosethorn grabbed it as yellow fluid ran out from under the glass top to drip on her gloves and arm.

"Stupid bleater!" Briar snarled.

He yanked Rosethorn away, sliding a hand underneath the tray to raise it until it was level. "Chufflewitted, festering—"

"Stop that," Rosethorn ordered, stripping off her gloves. "Take off your gloves."

"Rosethorn, he—"

A lordly voice cut him off. "You—out," Crane ordered. "Immediately."

The worker said, "I'm sorry. I'm so—" He put the tray on the counter and fled to the washroom.

"Let the gloves fall—we'll clean them up," a

friendly voice said in Briar's ear. It was Osprey, holding two fresh pairs. "Dedicate Rosethorn?"

"No harm done," claimed Rosethorn as she took the new gloves. Her face was pale. "It was scary, that's all. Briar, come put that anger to some use."

Briar followed her to the inner workroom, pulling on his new gloves. Watching Rosethorn go to her counter, he suddenly felt weak with fright. She had said there was no harm done, hadn't she? It must be true. She wouldn't let the tiniest drop of pox run between sleeve and glove, where it might touch her skin. Never. Besides, the spot on her forehead was still crimson. She didn't have the disease.

Or would it change color only when her body lost the fight to keep the pox from taking over?

He couldn't work like this. Steadying himself against his counter, Briar closed his eyes and practiced meditation breathing. He wanted to stop shaking before he even tried to handle his trays.

Niko and Tris halted where a pair of tunnels intersected. Tris felt the force of the water, thigh deep now, heavy on her barrier. She poured more strength into it, baring the ledge on which they stood and its counterpart across the intersection. With the gold shimmer in the water itself removed, they could see where the footprints continued after a jump from ledge to ledge.

Niko sighed. "I hope it's not too slippery over

there." He braced himself, then leaped across the canal, landing on the far side where the footprints resumed. Tris had to back up and run a few steps to get the speed to clear the canal.

"We were lucky at Winding Circle, I guess," Tris said grimly as they picked up the trail again. "All our water comes from wells on the other side of Wehen Ridge. None of this leaks through the stone of the ridge."

They passed more intersections and entered smaller tunnels, where they had no ledge to walk on. Tris shoved the sluggish liquid mess to either side, fiercely determined to avoid contact with it for as long as she could manage. She had to pity Niko. In here he was forced to walk in a stoop, trying valiantly to keep his head from touching the slime on the roof overhead.

Suddenly the trail ended in a broad, drippy blotch in the center of the tunnel and along a curved wall. Niko and Tris looked up. Immediately above that gold blotch was a barred rectangle of light: a grating. They could hear the rattle of wheels on cobblestones and a distant clock striking the half hour.

They had passed ladders to the street all during their expedition. There was one five yards ahead with a sign next to it that read LUCKY STREET & SHORT-SHANK WAY. Niko climbed up, opened the exit and looked around, then sank down a rung. "Stand back," he ordered Tris.

Confused, she did as she was told. Niko stripped off his heavy outer garments, dropping them into the sewer: only his mask, gloves, and street clothes remained. He then boosted himself up onto the street. "You do the same," he ordered, his voice a haunting drift from the light overhead. "Wait until you're almost out."

"Oh, joy," she muttered, panting as she struggled to climb the ladder. She tried not to remember that her three housemates would have clambered up like monkeys.

When Tris emerged, blinking, into the light, Niko stopped her. He'd removed his gloves and tossed them into the sewer. Now he pulled fresh ones from his satchel, giving a pair to Tris. As he placed the cover on the sewer hole, she looked around. They were not in the best part of town. Houses were jammed together, cobbles broken or missing in the street. A view of a towering wall between her and the sun told her they were in East District, near the wall that separated the poorest part of Summersea from the Mire.

Bodies lay on either side of the narrow rising way, many attended by rats. What faces she saw were covered with blue spots. Far down Lucky Street she heard a clanking sound, metal-shod wheels on stone. A wide, deep-bedded dray made its slow way uphill toward her. Workers in gloves, robes, and masks loaded the dead into it.

Those few who walked the hilly streets abroad were veiled or masked and moved with a quick, scuttling gait not unlike that of the rats. If they were puzzled at the emergence of a man and a chubby girl from the sewer, they kept it to themselves. Blue circles were painted on a number of doors to mark where the disease had struck. Fires burned on the corners. Homeless animals, their owners dead, roamed everywhere, digging through garbage in the hope of finding a meal.

A bony hand rested on her shoulder. "You can't think of that," Niko said. Of course he'd seen her eyes fill at the sight of the starving creatures. "We have to track down the disease. Time to renew the balm." He fished out the jar and, taking off a glove, dotted Tris's eyelids and his own. "Don't put your spectacles on just yet. Since we now trace not the magic as it became the plague, but the magic alone . . ."

He drew a glass vial from his satchel and opened it. As Niko touched the bottle's damp stopper to her eyelids and to the center of her forehead, above the diagnosis oil, Tris's long nose twitched. New scents—heavy, unpleasant, musty—poured into that sensitive organ. She was about to inquire when Niko said quickly, "You won't learn what goes into this one for a couple of years—some of the ingredients are poisonous. Don't even bother to ask. You can put your spectacles on."

She blinked as vapors from the new liquid made

her eyes sting. While Niko anointed his lids—she saw them blaze with her changed vision—she looked around. Scraps of magic glinted in corners and on door and windowsills, the remnants of luck and prosperity charms, love potions, and other small workings. A thin, blue-white cord stretched from a nearby sewer grating up the street.

Niko beckoned her; they followed the blue-white cord to a tall, ramshackle house nearby. The door, a blue circle painted around the knocker, was half off its hinges, which made it easy for Tris and Niko to enter. They stood in a dark and narrow hall, ankle deep in trash, facing a rickety staircase. All the doors on this story were as useless as the front door. Rats and insects fled into the empty rooms, trying to escape the light that now shone bright around Niko.

The blue-white cord led them up three flights of stairs. Tris guessed that this place had rented out rooms. It seemed that now most, if not all, of the building had been abandoned in the wake of the blue pox.

The staircase ended in a garret. The looters had apparently ignored this level. Maybe they don't like stairs either, thought Tris as she fought to catch her breath. There were only two apartments: the cord vanished through the closed door on one. Niko rapped hard, then tried the knob, only to find it locked. He sighed.

"We should have brought a guard with us," he told

Tris. "Now I have to find one—why are you smirking at me?"

Tris drew a small, rolled-up cloth from her pocket. *Briar?* she called through their magical bond. *I need some advice.*

Briar was about to pick up a new tray. Now he stepped away from the stack and turned his attention to his friend. *You came to the right person*, he said with approval, inspecting the locked door through her eyes. *Smart thinking, to bring your picks.* That winter, in exchange for lessons in reading classic Kurchali, he had begun to teach her the art of lock picking. *Which pick do you need to start?*

The long, straight one? she replied, a bit unsure.

Good. Now, get close.

Tris knelt before the lock and let Briar help her through the rough spots as Niko watched, bemused. She only needed two picks before the lock gave and the door opened. A wave of rot-stench surged from the room inside.

"Someone died here," Niko remarked.

"If you hadn't told me, I might never have known." Tris's sarcasm was nearly lost in the croaking of her voice as she swallowed a mouthful of bile.

You don't need me for this, Briar told her. *Good hunting.*

Once inside, they had to take a moment to blink their vision clear: strips, sparkles, and blots of magic shone everywhere. Half of the large room was a

186

mage's workplace, with a small herb garden in the window, bottles and boxes of ingredients perched on the shelves that lined one wall, a counter littered with jars, mortars, crystals of all shapes, and boxes of candles and ribbons. Another wall held twenty or so books. A meager hearth served for cooking as well as heat, and the pots and pans that hung from hooks around it had seen better days. A wooden trunk also served as a table. There was a footstool and three chairs, all in need of patching.

A tiny bedchamber opened off that room—Niko looked in and closed the door. "Our mage is dead," he said grimly. "Maybe that's best. Once her role in this was discovered, I think no power on earth could have kept her safe. People would have wanted vengeance."

"What if the past-viewing spell doesn't help us find out what we need to know?" Tris asked, worried.

"Somewhere in here is her journal or workbook. The past-viewing spell ought to show us where it is, and in turn it will tell us what she did." Niko sighed. "Are you ready to help me?"

Tris nodded. They had done this kind of spell once before, to find out why the Bit Island watchtower had exploded. Remembering how they had worked it, she threw a rope of power to Niko, letting him draw on her strength as well as his own. With her improved magical vision, she saw the power that jumped from his fingertips as a series of lightning-bright threads. The threads wove themselves into a circle around

Niko and Tris, then spread to enclose them in a globe of cobwebs that blazed like the sun. Tris shut her eyes, hoping to blot out the too-bright image, only to find the magic was still visible, though not the room. Sighing, she opened her eyes in time to see Niko make two cuts, one to each palm. He let the blood drip. It entered the spell-webs and raced through them, making them vanish. Now they saw the ghostly image of a short, dark-haired woman at the counter. From each of five bottles she dropped liquid onto five pieces of—

"That looks like bacon," she muttered.

Niko squinted for a better look. "It *is* bacon."

The woman made a note in a journal, watching the raw meat intently. One strip turned green and fell apart. One crinkled and turned yellow. A third liquefied. The remaining two turned black as coal, as if they had been cooked for much too long.

From the way she reacted, the dark-haired woman was furious. She flipped to an earlier page in her journal and crossed out what looked like recipes with angry slashes of her pen. She tugged her hair, hit the counter, and burst into tears. At last she stoppered the glass vials and put them in a covered basket. Something then made her pause.

She drew a purse through an opening in her skirt and upended it into her palm. A few copper coins spilled out. She stared at them, lips moving—counting, Tris guessed.

"No," whispered Niko, "you dolt, stop and think. There are reasons why the law says magical things must be disposed of at Winding Circle."

The woman counted her money again, then stared at her basket. Opening it, she removed the vials and emptied them into a wooden bowl. She closed the journal, tied a ribbon that glowed with magical symbols around it, and reached into the shelves in front of her, groping. The shelves swung open to reveal a hidden compartment. She set the journal there and closed it. Bowl in hand, the mage walked through Tris, opened a ghost door, and passed through the real one, out of their sight.

"Stupid," whispered Niko, as passionately angry as Tris had ever seen him. He stalked over to the shelves and reached under one, searching for the catch to the hidden compartment. "Stupid, stupid, stupid!"

"She just got rid of a potion that didn't work," protested Tris. When his search proved fruitless, she boosted herself onto the counter and thrust her smaller hand behind the bottles. She was interested to see that they were glued into place, never meant for use in the dead mage's work. Finding the catch, she tugged, and the shelf door swung open. She dropped to the floor as Niko removed the journal.

"She dumped five magically enhanced fluids that had not been properly neutralized," Niko rapped back. "With no thought of how they might interact with anything else. The fee charged to handle these things is small. Gods of light and knowledge save me from coin-pinching lackwits!"

"She was that tight with a copper." Tris and Niko turned. A bleary-eyed old woman leaned against the door of the other garret room outside. "Mind, she had to watch her money. Her work wasn't very good." Sly glee ran over the woman's puffy face. "Stands to reason, don't it? If she was any good, she wouldn'ta lived here with the rest of us poor folk."

"If you will excuse us," Niko said stiffly, holding onto the dead mage's journal. "We have no time to waste."

Tris ran down the stairs at a fast trot. Niko came after her. A voice drifted eerily down the stairwell: "Does this mean the curse on them that breaks into her place is gone?"

Crane was so limp with shock and disgust that Briar expected him to wilt into a heap. "Ah," the Air dedicate said in a tone so mild he might have been talking of spring rain. "All this—all this for a nostrum to help women to reduce their weight."

Rosethorn ran her finger over a page in the dead woman's journal. "This—Eilisa Pearldrop"—she said the name with raw sarcasm—"wanted to create a potion to consume body fat, making it dissolve in wastes and in sweat. It wouldn't hurt if the person who used it had little appetite as well. So the fever was built in, and made resistant to willowbark. Of course. Who would want to pay for a very expensive weight loss potion that would be made useless the first time you drank willowbark tea for a headache?" She looked at Niko and Tris, scrubbed and gowned for entry into Crane's realm, and shook her head. "It never would have worked. And she writes that the dark rash was a side effect she couldn't get rid of."

"So she dumped it illegally in the sewer, where it combined with the city's muck, to give us the blue pox," said Niko wearily. "Whichever of us enters the country of the dead first should locate her and tell her what she wrought."

"All this for money," whispered Crane. Looking at him, Briar thought that only people who were born rich had such a low opinion of money. "The death of hundreds," Crane went on, "from a pursuit of wealth and a reluctance to spend."

"She didn't have that much to spend, from the look of it," muttered Tris.

"And cursing her now or in the afterlife won't bring us closer to a cure," said Rosethorn. "Crane, let's split these notes of hers up between us and brew her recipes. Let Briar keep trying the magic-blockers we gave him this morning on the trays."

"Done," replied Crane. To Niko he said, "You told me I could have Trisana."

"Perhaps she needs a day to recover," suggested Niko, but Tris was already shaking her head. "Well, then, she's yours." He sighed. "I should report this to Moonstream and the duke."

"I do not envy you in the least," Crane said absently, beckoning to Tris. He said to her, "Since we do not wish to keep the book where it might get stained or torn, copy that female's recipes for all five potions while Rosethorn and I set up." He seemed to have forgotten that Niko was still there. "Give Rosethorn her copies. Then—"

Briar returned to his work. After Tris and Niko had left for the city, Rosethorn and Crane replaced all of his additives with new ones, each made to react to magic. He wanted to refill the cabinets that had been emptied that morning: those vacant shelves seemed like a reproach.

Niko stopped beside him on the way out. "How goes all?" he asked quietly.

"Fine," Briar said, trying not to think of that morning's spill.

"What happened there?" inquired Niko. He motioned to the outer workroom. "I see three layers of cleansing spells, all strong and very fresh."

Briar stared at him, startled. "Don't your eyes ever hurt you?" he wanted to know. "If you can see so much?"

Niko shrugged. "One grows accustomed."

Briar snorted. "You sound like Crane."

"Dear gods, anything but that," Niko whispered with a crooked smile.

"We had a spill of pox essence," Briar said. "They wanted to make sure they cleaned it all up." Curious, he asked, "Did *you* see it? The magic in the blue pox?" While Crane and Rosethorn read through the journal, Osprey had given Niko the tour, showing him even the contents of the distilling jars.

"Yes, but I wonder if I would have noticed it, had it not been pointed out to me. The sewer diluted Pearldrop's fluids so much that her small power is only a ghost within the disease. You and Tris did well to spot it—very well."

Briar shook his head, blushing at the rare compliment. Niko was hard to please. "I might not've had the nerve to say anything."

"You had the nerve to suggest Tris might be of use." Niko hesitated, then said, "Take care of yourself, Briar. Bringing you here was one of the best ideas I ever had."

It was as well he left then. Briar couldn't think of anything to say.

"First change," Rosethorn said cheerfully, coming over. Leaning past him, she erased the name of a test fluid they had started to use just hours before and wrote in a new one. Rubbing out the number one next to *Variation*—they had switched to numbers after the discovery that magic was a factor—she put the number two. "Let's get to it," she told Briar.

Before she turned away, he glanced at the diagnosis spot on her forehead. It was still there, still red.

194

Relieved, he went to ask Osprey where he would find powdered jade.

With the discovery of Pearldrop's weight-losing potions, the atmosphere in the greenhouse changed for the better, despite the fact that the workers were even busier. Briar might almost have said he was enjoying himself. All along he'd thought that, as exhausted and nervous as the greenhouse staff was, they had the best of it. They weren't nursing the sick and the dying, or being pressured like Crane and Rosethorn to find a cure. The helpers only had to do their jobs well.

One sign that things had improved came on the third day after Tris and Niko returned from the sewers. A tray slipped from Briar's hold as he carried it to his worktable. He jumped back quickly enough that he wasn't spattered with pox or shattered glass, then braced himself for Crane's wrath and that pointed finger. Rosethorn clenched her hands in her gloves, her eyes daring Crane to dismiss Briar. Crane didn't even look at her. His eyes rested on the spill as Osprey's crew came running to mop up, rose to Briar's face, then slid to the slate on which the boy's ever-changing instructions were written.

"Trisana, have you the list of supplies Rosethorn and I require from temple stores?" he inquired.

Tris made a face—she'd tried to get him to call her by her nickname, without success—and held up a slate.

Crane took it. "Briar, memorize this, scrub out, then collect these materials. Get everything, mind. If the people at stores do not have the amounts we require, they must promise to bring the rest with all due speed. The spill should be cleaned up by the time of your return." He held the slate out to Briar.

"You're not getting rid of me?" the boy asked, shocked.

"I believe there are ten silver astrels at stake on the date of your dismissal. I do not approve of gambling; therefore, no one shall win money from my dismissal of you. Take this list, and go—but remember to come back."

Briar did as he was told. Osprey went with him. "He *must* like your work," she commented admiringly as she gathered the special washes needed for a pox spill. "Guess I'd better return Tris's silver astrel, if he's on to the betting."

"May as well give me back my wager on Tris getting the boot," said the boy gloomily. "If he won't get rid of me, there's no way he'll rid himself of her."

"I noticed," Osprey told him drily. "If she wasn't already Master Goldeye's student, I'd be plenty worried, believe me."

Once Briar returned, he was put back to his former job. Nothing more was said about his accident.

That evening, just as Osprey announced it was time to close, a deep, emerald-green light dawned at Rosethorn's worktable. Briar saw its reflection in the glass and polished stone around him and turned, looking for the source. The light grew brighter and brighter, silhouetting Rosethorn's body.

"Crane, remember that change you suggested, switching from bloodstone to hematite?" she asked in a calm, ordinary voice. "You may have something."

"In combination with—?" He walked over to observe what she had done, as calm as she. Tris danced from foot to foot behind them, trying to see. Osprey was more dignified, but she too was trying to bend around Crane's side for a better look at Rosethorn's worktable. Briar went to Tris's chair and climbed it. Now he had a perfect view.

In the tray before Rosethorn, light blazed from a column of wells. "Juniper and yarrow, three parts, to one part wisteria oil," Rosethorn said, answering Crane's inquiry.

"Wisteria. Ah. That would explain the extravagant effects." Crane turned and looked down his nose at Osprey and Tris. Seeing Briar on the chair, he raised his brows.

Rosethorn covered her tray with its glass top and turned around. "Oh, for Mila's sake, calm down. It's just the first key." The outer workroom staff had crowded into the doorway to see what the fuss was about. Rosethorn told them, "It looks extravagant because it lit up, but we're still a long way from a cure. We must find thirty-six keys, by our reckoning." Crane nodded agreement.

Nonetheless, there was excited chatter in the washroom. When they all emerged from the greenhouse, Briar and Tris were invited to join the novices at the main dining hall. Rosethorn nodded permission. She and Crane wandered around the greenhouse to Crane's usual office, talking softly.

The next morning Rosethorn came over to Briar's table, he assumed to make that day's first change to his slate of instructions. Instead she rested a hand on Briar's shoulder. *I need a favor,* she told him mind-to-mind. *My own magical reserves are low—I must be tired, because I'm not replenishing overnight as I should.*

You need some of mine, Briar replied silently. *Sure. You look tired.*

Just once it would have been nice if you had been gallant and said I never looked better, she informed him. He knew she smiled under her mask because he could see the corners of her eyes crinkle up.

He ran a thick vine of his power through the point where her palm rested on his shoulder, letting his magic spill into her. He had plenty. His job entailed no use of it, while Rosethorn and Crane had been pouring theirs into experiments.

You want me to tap my shakkan? he asked silently, when she stopped the flow between them. *I can call it to me here.*

No, she said, *though I appreciate the offer. Keep the*

shakkan *in reserve. If you make too much use of it, you'll get lazy with your own power.* She stopped, then remarked, *Well, well. I believe* someone *has found the second key.*

She turned, taking her hand from Briar's shoulder. Briar did the same and squinted against the white radiance that poured around Crane's lean figure. Tris had turned away, shading her eyes with one arm. Osprey and her crew ran in and burst into applause.

"It is only the second key," said Crane, his voice pleased. "There are many more to go—though I admit, it is good to see we are moving in the proper direction at last."

"Osprey, is there tea?" asked Rosethorn. "I need a large mug with plenty of honey. Oh—before that, a small cup of willowbark tea." Osprey nodded and went to get the cups herself: a pot of the daily mixture and a pot of willowbark were always on the brew in the outer workroom, in a spelled cabinet that also kept the cups and honeypot from harm. Those teas received as much respect as the magical research texts. None of them could have endured an entire day without tea.

"Willowbark?" Briar whispered, so only Rosethorn could hear.

She rubbed her forehead on the back of her glove. "Try squinting through lenses and running magic through all sorts of crystals. See how long it is till *you* get a headache," she said with her old rude spirit.

"Crane, let me see." She went over to examine what Crane had done.

Briar frowned. Rosethorn never got headaches, even while laboring in her garden under the summer sun. He watched her walk to the center of the room, away from the counters, to lower her mask and gulp the willowbark tea that Osprey brought, making a face at its bitterness. She traded that empty cup for the other, sweeter tea she'd requested.

She's lost weight, he realized. Why hadn't he noticed?

Crane approached to make a change to Briar's slate. The boy considered mentioning his worries and decided against it. Crane would simply look down his long nose and say that Rosethorn was perfectly able to look after herself.

And don't that show what *he* knows, thought Briar grimly, fetching a new tray.

Some time later he heard Osprey utter the welcome phrase, "Lunch." He was putting things away when Rosethorn said, "No, thanks, Osprey. I'm not hungry."

"You know better," Crane announced sternly. "You—gods defend us."

Briar looked to see what made Crane speak as he had. Rosethorn had turned to face the room, bracing herself on her counter with one hand. For a moment Briar knew only that something was wrong, though he wasn't sure what it was.

"Rosethorn, no," Tris wailed softly.

"Why is everyone staring?" demanded the woman.

Briar shut his eyes, then opened them. Immediately he saw the thing that had changed. The red thumbprint on her forehead had turned white.

Rosethorn saw it in their faces. "Oh, my," she said weakly. "It was that spill, I suppose. I wish we could make these clothes skintight!"

"No!" Briar cried, going to her. "No, it can't be. It can't! The spot would've turned color right then— wouldn't it?" he asked Crane, trying not to plead. "Our dots ain't fresh. We got 'em more'n a week ago, so they went stale, that's all."

Crane handed a piece of brightly polished metal to Rosethorn, who could then see for herself that her diagnosis spot had changed color. "Your magic?" he asked her, his voice emotionless. Briar wanted to kick him. Didn't he *care*, after all she'd done?

"I'd run low," Rosethorn said quietly. "My power kept it at bay—until now."

"Until now," Crane said. "So long as your body fought, and could fight, the oil would not react to the disease. I knew I should have refined that diagnosis oil, but we were pressed for time. . . ."

"Can't I stay?" Rosethorn asked him. "Surely I have at least a day's more work in me. The tea got rid of my headache."

Crane sighed. "My dear," he said, his voice regretful, "shall I get the orders with regard to a researcher who succumbs to a disease? They are in *your* writing."

"I hate it when you're right," she replied.

"I know," Crane told her. "If it makes you feel better, Lark will kill me for allowing this to happen."

"An *accident*," growled Tris. Like Briar she had come to stand near Rosethorn. "Just a stupid, stupid—" Her voice cracked. She was crimson behind her mask.

"Let me take her home," Briar said to Crane. "She ought to be in bed."

"She cannot go home—surely you are aware of this."

Briar stared up at the man, furious. Was that *kindness* in Crane's eyes? Who was he to go being kind to anybody, particularly to him or to Rosethorn?

The true betrayal came in her quiet, clear voice. "No matter where *I* end up, you will stay here."

"I won't!" snapped Briar. "Let them whiffenpoof Water Temple slushbrains have the care of you? Stay here putting a drip of this and a drab of that into a hundred stupid trays on maybe the side chance one of 'em'll creep us along a hair to a cure?"

"Yes," Rosethorn said firmly.

"I need you here."

He was hearing things, surely. He could have sworn Crane said he needed him.

The lanky dedicate sighed, and leaned against Rosethorn's worktable. "Your hands are steady. Your discipline over your power is such that no shadow of it changes the essence of the blue pox or of the additives. You keep your head in an emergency, for all that you speak wildly enough."

"I can't," Briar told Rosethorn softly, pleading. "Don't make me stay."

"What is more important, tending me—when the best nurses around the Pebbled Sea are here—or helping to find the cure?" she asked gravely. "If you go, they must train someone else for your job—and someone after that, and someone after that, since Crane will get rid of anyone new who looks at him cross-eyed."

"Unjust," drawled Crane.

"Absolutely right," said Osprey.

"He will lose time," Rosethorn continued, ignoring them. "Osprey will lose time. The best you can do for me is to keep working."

Tris sighed abruptly. She had been so quiet they had forgotten she was standing there. "Rosethorn, Lark says you're to wait until she comes. She and Sandry are going to Moonstream to see if they can take you home."

Briar wanted to hug the redhead. He kept himself from doing it, but just barely. Of course Tris would see that Lark would not want Rosethorn anywhere but home.

Anywhere but home, he thought again. There was something in the idea that grabbed his attention.

Of course. "You have to go home," he told

Rosethorn firmly. "You have to be near your plants and your garden, even if the garden's asleep. Remember Urda's House? Tris brought the *shakkan* and the ivy and herbs to make you feel better? Tris, tell Sandry to tell Lark that Rosethorn needs her plants."

Rosethorn looked at him sharply, then at Crane. "I forgot that living plants help."

"Join with ours, then," he said quietly. "You'll need as much strength as you can gather to fight this."

Rosethorn closed her eyes briefly. Briar felt tendrils of her power spread at lightning speed, weaving themselves in with the thousand lives on the other side of the tiled wall. He'd heard Rosethorn express dislike for Crane's greenhouse so often that it was almost funny to know she was getting strength from it now.

"It's still not the same as plants living and fading in their normal season," Rosethorn muttered, as if she had read Briar's mind.

"It is for those that flower all year in hotter climes," retorted Crane. "They are not even aware they are not in their home jungles."

Rosethorn rested her head on her hands. Now that she wasn't trying to pretend she felt normal, Briar could see how worn she was. For a moment a terrible fear rose in his heart. Quickly he thrust it into the very darkest corner of his mind.

Appealing to Rosethorn's own Green Man and

Mila of the Grain, he thought, Please, gods, keep her safe.

Crane and Tris returned to their work and Briar to his, though the boy kept one eye on Rosethorn. She sat at her own table, writing notes and tinkering with the tray she had been working on. She seemed determined to finish it, and Crane would not protest an activity that kept her quiet as they waited for word from Lark.

The Hub clock was chiming one in the afternoon when the word came in the form of Lark herself. Briar sighed with relief as she walked past him. Lark glanced at him and winked, then took Rosethorn's hand. "I have special passes signed by Moonstream and permission to take you back to Discipline, as long as you're freshly robed and masked after we leave here," she said briskly. To Crane she added, "It's not as if this thing goes easily from person to person. We'll have gloves, and masks, and Daja's coming—Frostpine said they were about done in any case. If you want to see my passes, you'll have to come out to look at them—I couldn't bring them through your washroom."

"I trust you, Lark," he said. "If you will now take her away, so we may get some real work done—?"

Onini bless me, thought Briar, calling on the goddess of flower sellers, I think he's teasing Rosethorn. No, he can't be!

Rosethorn stiffly got to her feet. "Just one thing, Crane," she said, an impish look in her eyes. She put a drop from an amber-colored vial on the tip of one gloved finger and drew a straight line down the cover on the first well in each row on her tray. They began to shimmer green at their bottoms. Slowly the light expanded and rose, until it filled each well, and flowed together on the spaces between them. "Here's your third key." Lark tried to put an arm around her friend's waist, but Rosethorn shook her head. "I can walk—I'm just a bit achy." To Briar she said, "Will you do as I asked? Will you stay here?"

Briar looked from her to Crane and Tris. If she's got Sandry and Lark and Daja tending her, she'll be all right, he realized. I *can* do her more good with Crane, helping him track down the cure.

Reluctantly he nodded.

"That's my boy," said Rosethorn. With Lark, she walked out of the workroom.

"Well," Crane remarked, and sighed. "We'll need to change things. Osprey," he called, raising his voice so she could hear it from the other workroom. "Who among your crew of professional jesters would you trust to run things in your place?"

Osprey stuck her head through the doorway. "In my place? Sir?"

"I think I really must have you in here," Crane told her. "You will do research during this crisis after all. Who will be effective in the outer workroom?"

Osprey turned. "Dedicate Acacia?"

Crane sighed gustily. Osprey looked back at him. "Trust me, he'll do fine."

Her teacher flapped a limp hand. "He had better. Give him your instructions, and then let us get busy. There is much to do."

As the Hub clock struck nine, Dedicate Acacia, a young man whose blue-black skin was accented by the pale, undyed material of his mask, robe, and cap, came to the doorway. He shifted from one foot to the other nervously.

"Honored Dedicate, we must close," said Acacia. "Actually, we are an hour late to close. I—"

"No," protested Briar fiercely. "We can't stop now! Rosethorn's sick—we have to keep working!"

"You can't," Acacia said gently. "No living thing could survive the cleansing steam. And everyone is weary."

"Tired people make mistakes," Crane informed

him. "If you have not learned that before now, commit it to memory."

Briar put stoppers in jars, furious. All the others could think of was supper and bed. Rosethorn was in trouble, might *die*, because they didn't care enough to really bear down and do the job.

A hand gripped his wrist as he was about to slam the door to the additives cupboard. "Stop it," Osprey told him very quietly, green eyes blazing over her mask. "You think Rosethorn's the only one in danger? Crane needs rest, what little he takes. He's up till all hours, reading those blasted notes and thinking of new ideas, and then he's here at dawn. So calm down and tell everyone good night."

She's right, Tris said through their magic. Briar had thought she was busy tidying up. He should have known she would hear so intense a discussion. *Did you stop to think what happens if Crane gets sick?*

Briar froze.

You didn't, Tris commented. She had turned to look at him. *Think about it now, and let's go wash. My eyeballs are dancing.*

Briar gave his work area a last check to ensure that everything was stowed in watertight cabinets, safe from the cleansing steam. Osprey had gone to speak to the outer workroom crew. Crane was lost in thought, gazing blankly through the glass wall at the fog that rose in the night air.

It all depended on Crane now, didn't it? He had

plenty of help, it was true, but the experience and the skull work would be his.

I don't even *like* this man, Briar thought, dismayed. I respect him, but I don't like him. And he don't like me.

The things I do for her, he told himself, and walked over to Crane. "You can stare and blink as well outside as in here," he reminded the dedicate. "And I want my supper, even if you don't."

Crane looked at him as if he had forgotten who Briar was. Then he shook his head as if to clear it. "True. Let us be off, then. We shall return all too soon."

It had been in Briar's mind to sit with Rosethorn. Lark would hear nothing of it. "Visit after you eat," she said firmly, thrusting Briar and Tris toward the table. "But not for long—you're going to bed. You cannot be muzzy when you work like this, you know. Some of the worst disasters in history came about because people were too weary to know they made errors." She brought covered supper plates that she'd kept warm on the hearth, while Daja poured out juice. "*She's* done nothing but scribble ever since I brought her home."

Briar, listlessly picking up a napkin, felt interest course through his veins like tonic. "She's doing notes?"

Symbols of health and protection gleamed silver

210

on Rosethorn's doorway, to keep sickness inside. They didn't capture sound, because Rosethorn called loudly, "You thought I would come home to languish? I have some things Crane should try. Come in after you finish."

Tris grinned at Briar.

He started to eat. He bet Crane would be glad of Rosethorn's notes for as long as she could make them. And as long as she *did* make them, Briar knew her thinking was still sharp, not fever-muddled. The blue pox might have fooled the diagnosis oil for a time, but it had a serious battle to fight if it wanted to munch up Rosethorn.

Once finished, he got his *shakkan* and took it to Rosethorn. "It's glad of company," he said cheerfully as she glared at him. She sat propped up on pillows as she wrote on a lap-desk. "It moped the whole time we went north last fall and lost a couple of twigs. I'll feel better if you'd just watch it."

"Of course," Rosethorn said tiredly. "I can see it's moping. If we're not careful, it could shed a needle. I don't need a nursemaid, young man, not even a green one."

Briar grinned. "You got one anyway."

"I *have* one anyway. Take this." She held out a waxed paper tube, spelled like the doorway to keep out disease. Briar accepted it with a gloved hand: at Lark's command, anyone who saw Rosethorn dressed as they might for Crane's workroom.

"Now go to bed," Rosethorn ordered. "I bet two silver astrels that Crane finds a cure before I show spots. That means you need to rest and help him win me money."

"Even if he don't approve of gambling?" Briar shook his head, glad she could joke.

Rosethorn grinned. "*Particularly* because he doesn't approve of gambling."

If Crane was glad to see Rosethorn's notes once they were carried through the washroom in their waxed tube, he hid it well. He read them, Briar noticed, but he directed Osprey to do the suggested work. Briar tried to watch Osprey, until he ruined a tray by losing track of what he'd added. After that, he kept his mind on his work.

The pace in the greenhouse changed. Acacia often came to ask Osprey things, while Crane spent more time advising Osprey than he ever had with Rosethorn. Osprey always had questions and needed to check almost every step with Crane, which maddened Briar. He wanted to order Acacia to show some backbone and Osprey to let Crane work. One day went by, then two, then three: every minute that Crane was distracted was a minute taken from Rosethorn's life. They had found no more keys since her last discovery. Each night, when the crew left the greenhouse, Briar looked for a steady bright glow over the wall between them and Bit Island, hoping not to see it. It was the fires in the vast pit where the dead were burned, and it was always there.

At midmorning of the third day, the clamor of tolling bells in Summersea got louder, making the glass on his counter wobble. Then Briar realized it wasn't city bells, but the Hub bell, that clanged so mournfully.

"What is it?" asked Tris. "What happened?"

"One of our own died," Osprey replied, making the gods-circle on her chest.

"Who?" asked Tris. No one knew. Neither Sandry nor Daja, caring for Rosethorn, had any idea of who it was.

That night, when Briar and Tris came home and looked in on Rosethorn, they found Lark with her. The women clasped each other's gloved hands; both had reddened, puffy eyes, as if they'd been weeping.

"Henna," Rosethorn said to Briar. "The fever. That cursed fever!"

"Her magic," Briar whispered numbly. "She said she always kept enough back to burn it out—"

"Except she didn't," Lark said bitterly. "Willow-water told me she was helping a couple of sick novices."

Briar stared at Rosethorn, frightened. Rosethorn's eyes were glassy; her lips were dry and peeling. She was feverish. It was as if death circled his teacher.

Quietly he poured a cupful of willowbark tea and brought it to her.

213

"I am so *sick* of this rubbish!" cried Rosethorn, glaring at him. "I swear, I'm going to float away in a sea of *horse* urine!"

"Oh, no, love," said Lark, taking the cup from Briar. "I assure you, horse urine is *much* more strongly flavored."

Rosethorn, Briar, and Tris stared at her in horror. "How—?" began Rosethorn.

"You don't want to know," Lark replied solemnly. "It's better to drink this."

Rosethorn stared at her, then drank the tea down.

Lark winked at Tris and Briar. "You just have to know how to talk to her."

Normally Rosethorn would have groaned and thrown a pillow at Lark. Tonight she only smiled and lay back. Lark nodded to the door with her head; Tris and Briar left.

It was the first time since her return from the greenhouse that Rosethorn had no notes to send back to Crane.

In bed that night, Briar dreamed he searched for Rosethorn in a foggy place, knowing she was there but unable to see her. The fear that she was lost—that she might be hurt, or worse—made it impossible to breathe.

He woke with a start, facedown in his pillow. His room smelled like night terrors and sweat without the *shakkan* to sweeten the air. Disgusted, he walked out

214

into the main room, dragging his blanket, and lay it on the floor next to the dog. Tris was curled in a knot before the gods' shrine in the corner, clutching her blanket to her chest. Briar covered her more thoroughly.

Sandry joined them a few minutes later with her own covers. Daja thumped down the stairs with hers. Hearing Daja, Lark came from Rosethorn's room and looked them over. "I'll get pallets in here tomorrow, if you want to do this," she said quietly. Daja, Briar, and Sandry—Tris had not woken—nodded.

Briar was just setting up the next morning when he saw white light shimmering in the shiny surfaces around him. Tris yipped with glee, clapping her hands. The boy turned.

Crane was removing a pair of trays from his personal cabinet, where he kept his experiments. They blazed hotly, marking the first breakthroughs since Rosethorn had gone. Once he'd put them on his worktable, Crane turned to Tris. "There is hardly a need for such enthusiasm," he drawled. "It was bound to happen at some point."

"But two of them!" Tris pointed out, refusing to be deflated. "Two!" Looking at Crane's drooping frame, the girl shook her head. "I'll be happy for both of us," she said, uncovering her inks.

The more emotional he feels, the limper he acts, thought Briar. Remembering his first encounters with

Crane he added, *Unless he's so furious he forgets he's nobility. It's like somebody taught him it's wrong to be excited.*

He reached for Sandry, who sat with Rosethorn that morning. *Two?* repeated Sandry, once Briar had explained the good news. *That's splendid.*

Briar frowned. There was a shadow in Sandry's mind.

No, don't! she cried, feeling him shift to look through her eyes. She covered her face, but it was too late: Briar had seen. Rosethorn was covered with dark spots.

Lark's gone for a healer, Daja told him magically. *We're to keep getting Rosethorn to drink things and to rub lotion where she itches. She'll be fine.*

Frightened as Briar was, Daja's calm solidity was a comfort. How could Rosethorn come to harm with her and Sandry there? She couldn't, of course, and things were starting to move in Crane's workrooms.

It's just a shame she lost her bet, is all, Briar told the two girls, explaining about Rosethorn's wager. *She threw out spots, but we don't have a cure.*

You will, Sandry told him firmly.

Stop gossiping and get to it, added Daja.

Briar obeyed.

The next key that day was Osprey's; the blaze of white light that announced it came just before noon. Crane developed another around two that afternoon. Osprey produced two more from Rosethorn's notes;

Crane brewed an eighth before they closed for the night.

"Good," Rosethorn said fuzzily when Briar reported to her. "Very good. Tell Crane when he's got something to try on patients, I'm his first volunteer."

Briar swallowed. "Are you sure that's a good idea?"

Rosethorn smiled, barely able to stay awake. "Before he reaches that point, there's a test fluid we made—actually, there's a set of ten fluids. I can't remember what we called it—"

"Human essence," said Lark. She had taken over from Sandry and Daja, and sat in a chair by the bed, knitting.

"That sounds right," agreed Rosethorn. "Crane will test cures on the essences before he tries real people. Once he does that, his first cures may not work for everyone, but they won't kill anybody either. They . . ." Her voice drifted off, and she slept.

"You know the disease better than I," Lark said to Briar. She leaned forward to hold Rosethorn's hand. "I take it this wandering and confusion is normal?"

Briar nodded. "It's the fever. We almost never lost anyone with spots. It was always after they faded, when the fever got out of control."

Lark reached out with her free hand and took his. "We'll all get through this," she told him solemnly. "It will end, and we'll be fine."

That morning Crane didn't wait until his workers had finished in the washroom, but scrubbed when they

217

did. Once inside, no one split off to begin their day's work. Crane, Osprey, Briar, and Tris led the way to the inner workroom as the rest of the staff crowded in the doorway near Briar's table. All eyes were on the cabinets where Crane and Osprey stored the previous day's experiments.

Gray and wet as it was outside, it could have been a sunny day once those cabinets were opened. Tray after tray blazed as they were brought out.

"Well," Crane remarked at last, when he'd looked it all over. "Well. Ten keys. Have you ever encountered a lock that needed so many, Briar?"

The boy shook his head emphatically, speechless. Hope was so thick in his throat that it half choked him.

"Now you have. A disease is the most complex lock there is," said Crane. "We have more keys to find, so if we might begin?" He looked at his staff. They disappeared into the outer room, eager to get started.

"What are you working on?" asked Rosethorn, holding out a thin hand.

Daja jumped, startled—she had thought Rosethorn was asleep. When the woman's fingers twitched, demanding, she blushed and passed her work over. She had been trying to shape copper wire to combine the signs for health and protection. She'd wanted to put it in a brass circle and hang it above the bed. For some

218

reason, though, when she added her magic, the metal twisted, jumping out of the pattern.

Rosethorn eyed the design. "Interesting. It might work better as a plant. If Briar built a trellis in this shape, we could grow ivy on it. You know why I hate plagues?"

The girl hesitated, confused by the abrupt change of subject. That was the fever, she realized. It made Rosethorn's mind skip about. "Why?" Daja asked.

"Most disasters are fast, and big. You can see everyone else's life got overturned when yours did. Houses are smashed, livestock's dead. But plagues isolate people. They shut themselves inside while disease takes a life at a time, day after day. It adds up. Whole cities break under the load of what was lost. People stop trusting each other, because you don't know who's sick."

"How did you get in with Crane?" Daja inquired, curious. "Picking apart diseases?"

"It was a game," Rosethorn confessed. "I was sent here to complete my novitiate. Crane was a novice too. We were the best with plants. A lady was visiting one day, and I worked out the ingredients in her perfume before Crane did. Except he wasn't Crane, then, he was just Isas, like I was Niva." Her eyelids started to droop, a sign she was tiring. Daja poured out a cup of willowbark tea and gave it to her. Rosethorn sipped, made a face, and continued. "We just went on from there. We'd make scents and give the other a day to figure out what was used and the amount. Then we worked out the ingredients in stews, and the dyes for the complex weavings that came in from Aliput. Then medicines—and then diseases. The temple sent us both to Lightsbridge for three years. I hated it, all those books and dead chemicals, powders, nothing alive. And they made so much of him as a count's son. . . ." She finished her tea and eased herself back. "So arrogant. So good at what he does. He's been a burr between my toes for years." She pulled the blanket up over her shoulders.

Daja set the empty cup in the bucket of things to be washed in boiling water and put the lamp behind a screen. She was about to try her work again when Rosethorn muttered something.

"What is it?" asked Daja. "Or are you walking in dreams again?"

"My boy. You three girls—look after Briar. When I'm gone."

Sandry and Tris would have argued passionately, refusing to admit there was a chance that Rosethorn might die. Daja was a Trader: they held it was mad to argue when the sick thought that Death approached. Denials only told Death here was someone who would be missed, Death's favorite kind of victim.

Daja did not protest. "We'll look after him forever," she promised.

"And tell him to mind my garden," whispered Rosethorn. She went to sleep.

Daja went back to her chair, but she couldn't work. Her eyes had gone blurry.

So many keys were found that day that Briar and Tris fumbled their way home, the afterimages of light-sprays still floating in their eyes. They were giddy with hope when they reached Discipline, eager to tell everyone what they had seen.

Their high spirits evaporated when they visited Rosethorn. She didn't know them. She was flushed with fever, and hallucinating. They heard her plead with her father to go to the harvest dance, and in a younger voice scold someone for tracking across her rows of seedlings.

Sandry, in the chair by the bed, smiled woefully at them. A piece of embroidery lay on her lap. When Tris picked it up, not wanting to look at the woman whose hands stirred restlessly on her blanket, she saw the beginnings of a needlework portrait of Rosethorn. She dropped it as if it were a hot coal.

More keys were found in the morning. When Acacia announced lunch, Crane gathered his staff together.

"Begin to pack the sample boxes in crates," he ordered. "If things go well, we shall only need to burn their contents, then melt down the boxes. Distill no

221

more blue pox samples for the present time. The five jars we have, as well as what is already in the trays, should suffice."

"We're done?" someone asked. Two more began to applaud.

Crane shook his head. "As far as I can tell, we have found all the keys to the illness. Now we formulate a cure. We have available a number of ways to cancel individual keys, which are different parts of the disease. These ways do not all work together. A bad combination of cancelers will kill a patient as easily as the blue pox. Also, different people react in different ways. Now we must devise the canceler blends that will treat the largest number of the sick."

"Some will die anyway?" whispered a man.

"We're mages, not miracle workers, Cloudgold," said Osprey tiredly. "Our strength has limits, and we don't have much time."

"I didn't *mean* anything by it," mumbled Dedicate Cloudgold. "I'm just a librarian."

"We are all tired," said Crane. "We shall be more tired still before we are done. If you will erase all of your variations, Briar?"

"*Everything?*" demanded the boy, startled.

"We begin on cures today," said Crane. "For that we shall need a clean slate."

Briar obeyed, but seeing that black rectangle bare of writing made him feel almost naked. As long as instructions were there, he knew they were doing something. He had fixed on the slate to keep from thinking.

An hour later, Crane lifted the slate down and chalked in new orders. Collecting all the materials he would need to create new additives, Briar whistled cheerfully. Once again he had things to do.

That night, Rosethorn's condition was the same.

Light filled the greenhouse workrooms the next day to announce effective blends of cancelers tested against trays full of blue pox. Several times Tris had to beg Crane to stop dictation, as she worked the cramps out of her writing hand. Osprey had moved to Crane's table, to help her teacher mix oils and powders for tests on the disease. Everyone in both workrooms protested a stop for lunch. They knew they were close and begrudged every minute not spent in blending and testing chemicals and herbal medicines.

At the day's end, Crane opened a cabinet at the end of his worktable, to reveal ten black glass bottles and ten dense black slabs. Someone had cut five wells three inches deep in each slab and polished the whole to a glossy finish. The bottles were sealed with layers of cloth and wax over a glass stopper. Everything shimmered with layers of magic and symbols written in power so intense it burned into Briar's and Tris's vision.

The black trays went to the outer workroom, where blue pox essence was put in each well. Once they were returned to Crane, he and Osprey unsealed the bottles. Acacia carried in a series of small cups, each big enough to hold a dram. Like the bottles and the stone slabs, they were written over with strong magical symbols.

"Briar," Crane said. "Your hands are the steadiest. If you will oblige me?"

Briar shook his head. "But I dropped a tray—"

"Once," Crane said drily. "And as often as you have made additions to the trays, you have not broken the lids, splashed the pox, nor dripped additives on your work area."

The boy stared at Crane, astounded. How closely had the man been watching him?

"If you please?" Crane asked, raising his eyebrows.

Briar looked at his trembling hands. This was even more important than the times he knew the Thief-Lord would starve him if he rang a single bell on the chuffle-dummy's pockets as he lifted their contents. This was more important than the risk of the docks or the mines if a hinge squeaked as he went for a jewel box. This might be Rosethorn's life.

"Right," he said, clenching his shuddery fingers into fists. "What do I do?"

Crane directed him to fill the cups, one for each bottle, with a liquid every bit as magically strong as anything he'd ever seen. Next he added the contents of the cups to the black stone wells. Osprey marked each slab with a glued-on patch of brightly colored cloth. Purple was for old men, lilac for old women.

Red was for men in their middle years, pink for women of that age. Olive-green was young men, yellow for young women, dark blue for boys, light blue for girls. Boy infants were black; girls were white.

"Eight years," Crane remarked softly as Briar measured and poured. "It took six of us eight years to blend these essences, to reduce the need to experiment on human beings. Xiyun Mountstrider, from Yanjing, died of breakbone fever in the third year. We thought we would never succeed without him. Rosethorn convinced us to press on. Ulra Stormborn went blind in the fifth year. First Dedicate Elmbrook took Ibaru fever and bled to death inside her skin in the seventh year, and we continued the work."

The thought of that kind of dedication made Briar feel small and untried. *I don't know if I could do that*, he confessed to Tris through their magic.

Me neither, she admitted.

"Now the first round of cures," said Osprey. While Briar poured the human essences, she had blended five different cures from her notes and Crane's. "Gods willing," she whispered, adding them to the liquids in the black stone wells. "Gods willing, these will be the ones."

That night they found Rosethorn's condition to be the same.

The cures were unsuccessful, as they all saw the next morning. Had they worked, Crane told his staff, the blue pox would have floated to the top of each well as a white oil. The workers scrubbed and boiled the black slabs while he and Osprey created five more cures. Briar once again measured out human essences; Osprey added the new medicines when he finished. Everyone went home, to wait.

Rosethorn was no worse, but no better. Her blue spots had begun to fade. The four young people sent Lark to bed. When she woke late that evening, they made her eat.

Briar wanted to cry when they reached the greenhouse at dawn, to find these cures hadn't worked either. Tris did cry. When the slabs were clean, they did it all again.

Returning home before sunset for the second day in a row, they found that Frostpine sat with Rosethorn. Lark and Sandry had returned to making protective oils and working them into cloth for masks and gloves. The smith went home around midnight, as Daja sat watch over their patient.

Several hours before dawn, Little Bear's yapping roused everyone. Briar lurched out of his blankets to see what had set the dog off; Lark, Sandry, and Tris sat up, blinking. Daja stuck her head out of Rosethorn's room. Opening the front door, Briar found Crane about to knock. The tall dedicate looked as exhausted as a man could look. He clutched a flask in one hand.

"One of the cures worked," he told the boy in a

croak. "I told Osprey to create more and try it on the other volunteers at the infirmaries. I want to administer this dose to Rosethorn myself."

Briar let him in.

Frostpine arrived halfway through the morning and stayed, helping with chores. Crane came and went. He checked the other cure volunteers, all temple people who'd caught the pox while tending the sick, looked in on Osprey and the greenhouse crew, then returned to Discipline to watch over Rosethorn. Once people knew he was at the cottage, runners delivered the latest reports on the progress of the volunteers to him there.

Rosethorn was doing better. Her sleep was more natural; she didn't babble. She was cool to the touch and dewed with sweat. Lark felt good enough about her progress to draw everyone out of her room after lunch and let her sleep without a guardian nurse.

Fortunately it was Daja, the most even-tempered of them, who looked into Rosethorn's room late that afternoon. What they heard made them all go still, at the table or seated on the floor, their hands freezing on makework tasks.

"*Enough!*" Rosethorn's voice was a sandpaper-rough growl. "The next one who . . . who *peers* at me is going to die in a dreadful way! Either come in or stay out!"

Daja blinked, then murmured, "Stay out," and retreated.

Briar sighed. "Ah, the sweet birds of spring," he said blissfully. "I hear their glorious song."

Lark ran to her own room and slammed the door.

Rosethorn began to cough. Crane stood and went into her room.

A few minutes later, Frostpine asked, "Do you think she's killed him?"

"It's too quiet for murder," offered Briar in his best criminal judgment. "And he'd yelp more if she was mauling him."

"We'd better check," said Frostpine somberly. He and the four young people looked into the sickroom very cautiously. Crane sat beside Rosethorn's bed, accepting a cup from her. Rosethorn heaved a shuddering sigh and fought to sit up.

"More?" Crane asked, offering the water pitcher. His manner was as nobly elegant as ever.

"Willowbark, I think," Rosethorn said in a croak. She cleared her throat and tried again. "Please." Her quick brown eyes caught her audience. "Something for you?"

"No," replied Frostpine.

"No? Then go away. You too," she informed Crane.

He rose, poured her a cup of willowbark tea, then swept her an elegant bow. He ruined the effect by adding, "Don't laze about too long. We must go at the blue pox, find out just how so deadly a variation was made, then write a paper to present in Lightsbridge."

"I'll try not to laze," Rosethorn promised, and drank her tea. "I would like to see Lark, though."

"Shoo, shoo," Crane said, sweeping his hands—and Frostpine, and the four—ahead of him until all had left the room. He rapped on Lark's door. "She wants you," he called.

"Coming," Lark replied, her voice nearly as clogged as Rosethorn's.

Crane looked at Briar and Tris, arms akimbo. "I could use both of you," he said. "There are problems with the cure's effect on older and younger patients—we must experiment with those. For that, since time is precious, I would prefer that you sleep nearby, in the Air dormitories."

"I'll tell Lark," Sandry offered. She had been crying, though none of the four could remember when.

"Time to go," said Crane. "The sooner we begin, the sooner we are done."

There was still a great deal of hard work before they could announce a cure to the frightened city. Teenagers, the very young, and the old did not fare as well as adults of Rosethorn's age. Adjustments were made. Crane requested—and got—volunteers among the victims in Summersea, those with no magic whatsoever. He and his staff worked around the clock. Briar was vexed not to see Rosethorn, but getting a cure to Summersea was important. Hundreds had died and more were dying in the city; no one wanted those numbers to rise for even an hour longer if they could help it.

At last, five days after Rosethorn began to mend, they gave their cures to the Water Temple, which began to make them in the huge amounts needed in Summersea. Crane sent Briar and Tris home. "There will be a meeting in a week or two," he explained. "We learn better as we review what happened and what might have been done instead. Some of the discussion will be impossible for you to follow, but your observations will be of use."

"Which means what?" Briar asked Tris as they plodded home. The day was warm, almost summery. Time to start hoeing, he thought, seeing green shoots in the gardens around the buildings.

"He might learn something and we might learn something," Tris replied.

"That's what I thought he meant. Why doesn't he come out and say so?"

Tris blinked at him. "I thought he did."

"Oh, you're no help."

The minute they entered Discipline, they looked in on Rosethorn. She was drowsing, her cheeks flushed, one hand on the *shakkan*. Someone had placed more pillows at her back, so that she was half sitting. Lark was in the chair beside the bed, worrying her fingernails. When she saw Briar and Tris, she put a finger to her lips for silence and got up.

The rustle of her habit woke Rosethorn, who brushed Lark's sleeve with her fingertips. "I'm all right," she murmured, and coughed. The cough went

231

on and on, thin and high; she had no chance to catch her breath. Lark picked a cup off the bedside table and held it to Rosethorn's lips, steadying her.

Somehow Rosethorn drank what was in the cup. Her coughs faded, slowly. Finally she nodded, and Lark helped her to ease back.

"Pesky thing," whispered Rosethorn. "The cough, I mean." She began to hack.

"Rest," Lark said when Rosethorn was at ease again. "Don't talk."

Rosethorn nodded and closed her eyes.

Tris pried Briar's fingers from her arm. Unknowingly, he'd gripped her tightly enough to bruise.

Lark shooed them out and closed the door behind her. Briar took the cup from her hand, exploring its contents with his magic. He recognized Capchen chestnut and syrup of poppies.

"Poppy?" he whispered, horrified. "How'd she get so bad she needs poppy?" He turned to Daja, who cut designs in metal sheets at the table. "You told us she did fine!"

Daja's eyes were bloodshot. "You asked yesterday morning. I said she still had that cough."

"We didn't know," Lark told Briar, drawing him away from Rosethorn's door. "Rosie started to complain she couldn't breathe lying down, so we raised her and sent for a healer. Grapewell told us to make this up—he said it would ease the cough. And it does, for a while."

"Didn't he do anything? Didn't he have magic? Didn't you tell them it was for her?" demanded Briar. Something in Lark's eyes scared him badly.

"The healers are at the last of their strength, I bet," said Tris. "They've got to be careful with how they spend it. And maybe her body resists whatever they do. Osprey says that happens a lot, when people keep getting treated with magic."

Lark nodded.

Briar stared at Tris. How could she be so cold? This was Rosethorn in trouble, not a street rat, not some pampered lady who thought she was dying when she sneezed.

Tris's gray eyes met his, and Briar stepped back. There was something in them that made even him a little afraid. She had learned to grip her feelings: that didn't mean she had no feelings at all.

"Sandry's looking for a healer," Lark told Briar. "Someone with more juice in him than Dedicate Grapewell." She didn't even smile at the almost-pun. "Rosie's fever's up again—that willowbark tea might as well be water." Her fingers trembled. "She may have pneumonia. Grapewell listened to her chest, and I know he didn't like the sound. I listened early this morning. It's crackling, like bacon on the stove."

"Where's the willowbark?" asked Briar. "I'll give it a boost."

"On her windowsill," Lark replied.

Briar went into Rosethorn's room and found the

233

teapot. He was so intent on pouring magic into its contents, raising the willow's power as much as he could, that he didn't hear Rosethorn at first. It was only when he poured the tea into a cup and turned around that he realized she'd been calling, her voice hardly more than a squeak.

"Sorry," she apologized when he came to her. "If I talk louder, I cough."

"So don't talk," he ordered sternly. "Drink this." He helped her to sit up as Lark had done. The hard knobs of her spine pressed into his shoulder. She was too thin! What did she have to fight pneumonia with?

Rosethorn pushed the cup away. "Tired," she squeaked. "But sleep doesn't rest me much." She pressed against his shoulder, letting him know she wanted to lean back. "Crane?" she asked when she was comfortable.

"Stupid me," he muttered, taking her hand. *This way we don't have to risk you coughing*, he began, and stopped, horrified. Her power, vastly greater than his, was down to embers, and fading.

Out, she said firmly, and tugged her hand from his. "You don't want to be tangled with me, if . . . you just don't," she squeaked, her fever-bright eyes holding his. "Go. Let me rest."

Briar ran from the room to find Sandry talking to Lark, hanging on her teacher's arm as she panted. She'd been running. "—two to three healers each, and they won't budge," she said, gasping. "They're brewing

234

cures and watching whole wards and everyone else is in Summersea. *Everyone!* I told them how sick she is, but they said unless we bring her in they can't see her. And Lark, it's all second-raters here, I checked. They figure most of our people are mages to start with, so—" Daja pushed a cup of water at Sandry. The noble released Lark and grabbed it, gulping the contents.

"The strongest healer-mages have gone to Summersea," Lark finished grimly. "Well, she's too badly off—second-raters won't do."

"She's dying," Briar announced, his voice shaking. "I looked inside her. She needs the best they got, Lark."

"But you have to be wrong—she was fine yesterday morning," argued Daja.

"Except she never lost the cough. There's people in the infirmaries who are all better—they're going home," Sandry reminded Daja.

Tris protested, "Briar's not a healer, you could be wrong—"

"Almost all her magic is gone," he said flatly. "Clean gone."

Lark held up a hand for silence. They gave it, letting her think. Sandry watched her, knowing how dire the situation was. Only yesterday she had seen Lark work her most powerful charms to keep Rosethorn safe. Not two hours before Tris and Briar had returned, when Sandry had brought fresh linens to the sickroom, she had discovered Lark weeping, her

235

charms in her lap. All of them had fallen to pieces, unable to work in the face of Rosethorn's disease.

"Well," Lark said at last, "I'll have to find Moonstream, that's all."

"Moonstream?" asked Daja. "She'll order a healer to come?"

Lark shook her head. "She *started* as a healer. I bet she's at full strength. I'll track her down. That may be difficult." She looked at the four. "One of you will stay with her at all times? Alert, and on guard?" They nodded. "Fetch one of our healers if she gets worse." Her face hardened. "I don't care what you do to persuade them to come."

That, more than anything, told them how frightened Lark was. To threaten a healer . . .

We'll just hope it doesn't come to that, Sandry remarked through their magic. *Hope* really *hard*—

Because if it does come to that, we will *get one here*, Daja said with grim promise.

Lark shook out her habit. "Whatever happens, if she—" The woman swallowed, her mouth trembling. "If she actually goes, *don't put your magic in her.* Under *any* circumstances. You can't come back from that. No power can bring you back. Do you hear me?"

The girls all nodded vigorously.

"Moonstream," Lark said firmly, and left the house.

Briar's tea brought Rosethorn's fever down briefly. It never touched her cough. She continued to doze. He sat with her first, watching intently, praying to any gods that might listen. He would not fail Rosethorn as he had Flick.

An hour and a half after her departure, Lark returned, leading a horse. "Moonstream's in the city. We sent a messenger bird to Duke's Citadel, just in case, but her assistant doesn't believe she's there. I'm going to look. Crane's with me, and Frostpine and Kirel. We'll split up once we reach the Mire." Tris looked outside and saw the men waiting there, all on horseback. Lark continued, "I found Dedicate Sealwort at the main infirmary. He'll be here as soon as he can, to sit with her."

"Go," Sandry urged. "Go, go."

"Start praying," whispered Daja as Lark and the men rode off.

Sandry was on watch the first hour after Lark went to the city; Tris was next. Rosethorn dozed. Her fever began to rise during Tris's hour, but Briar was afraid to give her more willowbark. Too much could normally irritate the stomach; he had no way to know if willow laden with all the power he could call to it might not do more serious harm.

The day went from warm to hot, an early hint of summer. Sandry went into her room, keeping the door open. At first she embroidered—later she napped. Daja was up and down the attic stairs, tending both the house altar and the incense and candles on her own small family shrine. Each time she checked her candles, she prayed, asking the spirits of her drowned parents and siblings not to let Rosethorn into the ships that carried the dead to paradise. Briar dozed at the table and checked on Rosethorn every few minutes. He knew he irritated Tris, who was officially on duty, but for once the hot-tempered girl kept her silence.

At last Tris came out of Rosethorn's room and poked Briar's shoulder. He woke.

"*Now* it's your turn," she informed him.

"Thanks," he muttered. "That Sealwort—he still ain't here." Before he went in, he poured a dipper of water over his head and face. It helped to wake him. The warm day had acted almost like poppy syrup on a boy who was short of sleep.

Rosethorn looked no better. When her lips parted, he could hear the crackle of her lungs. Her pulse was rapid and thin under Briar's fingers, her breaths slow and draggy. She stirred as he took her pulse and looked at him.

"Something to drink? Water or juice?" he asked, hopeful.

She shook her head.

"Come on," he insisted. He raised her and put a cup of water to her lips.

She sipped, then turned her face away. "I just want to sleep," she said in that scary, breathless voice. "So tired."

The chair was not a comfortable piece of furniture; he suspected Lark chose it for that reason. The back rungs pressed his spine. The wooden edge of the seat dug into the tender muscles behind his knees. There was nothing to read, and he'd brought nothing to work on.

Come to think of it, he hadn't so much as stuck his head into Rosethorn's workroom in weeks. Rising quietly, he went to the window. Before the workshop had been built, that window would have granted him a view of the road and the loomhouses. Now he viewed shelves and counters in disorder. Briar winced and turned away. There was plenty for him to do there, once things calmed down.

He padded back to the chair and sat for a while more. With no window to the outdoors, the room was stuffy. He should open the workshop windows when he finished here, to get a breeze going. . . .

He dozed, then jerked awake. How could he sleep in that chair? Wrapping his fingers lightly around Rosethorn's hand for comfort, Briar fought with his eyelids. They drooped. He yanked them open. They fell shut as if weighted. He ought to ask Daja to take over.

No. Rosethorn was his teacher. His sister, his friend . . .

A sound woke him, a strangled gasp. He thrashed and fell off the chair. Rosethorn surged from her pillows, eyes starting from her head, clawing at her throat.

Seizure. The word came from nowhere. Seizure, she was having a seizure—

She was turning blue. Blue, from lack of air.

Sandry raced in, looked, and screamed for Tris and Daja. *How long?* she mind-spoke, frantic. *How long has she been at this?*

Don't know! he retorted, and grabbed Rosethorn's hands. He felt her mind and magic pull away, no, *fall* away. She dwindled in his power's eye, as if she had gone over a long, long drop.

He did remember Lark's warnings about being with her as she died. He remembered and ignored them. Gathering himself, he leaped after Rosethorn, seized a trailing rootlet of her power and clutched it tight.

Tucking himself into a ball, Briar Moss plummeted after his dying teacher. Desperately he threw back an arm-vine, twining it around the towering magic hidden inside the *shakkan*.

Sandry roused to a thud and a gagging sound. She scrambled into the sickroom in time to see Briar thrust a sun-bright flare of power into Rosethorn, a shining bridge to a place filled with shadows. That place had opened a door inside Rosethorn.

"Tris! Daja!" she screamed, and asked Briar how

240

long Rosethorn had been unable to breathe. He didn't know, and he didn't care. He was gone, chasing the person he loved best into the shadows. He threw out a snaking vine of magic in his wake, letting it coil around the *shakkan*.

Sandrilene fa Toren took a deep breath. She too remembered Lark's warning, but there were other issues here. Death had seized her parents and the nursemaid who was like a mother to her. It was time to make a stand. Death would not take Rosethorn. Death would not take Briar. And wasn't it lucky she'd had some days of rest once the cure was found?

She knotted her magic briskly around Briar's swiftly fading power and jumped into the shadows in his wake. As the darkness pulled her from the sickroom in Discipline cottage, someone—two someones—grabbed her hands.

Who anchors? Tris wanted to know. She briskly sank hooks of lightning into Sandry as the noble's power stretched, a rope between the three girls and Briar. *I don't know if the* shakkan *will be enough to hold us all.*

Who else anchors? Daja inquired calmly. *As if you had to ask.* Her power was at full spate, restored from her magical workings with Frostpine. Some of it she hurled into the ground like a lance, feeling it shoot through earth and rock, spreading in an almost plant-like way. She solidified that system, making roots of

241

stone. The other end of her magic she threw around Tris, wrapping her tight.

Sandry drew strength from the chain of girls, feeling lightning roar through her magical self. Shadows jumped back as she bore down on the streaking comet that was Briar. Knotting lightning to shape a net, she threw it over the boy and pulled, until the net caught on the center of Briar's power and held. He was not going to die. They would not *let* him die.

Briar knew the girls had him, had anchored him in the living world. He was glad to have their company and their strength, but if they thought he would come home without Rosethorn, they were wrong. He couldn't let her go. He'd allowed Flick to die—wasn't that failure enough for anybody?

Things were strange, where he was. Sounds and images that were haunting and familiar coursed through him and were gone before he could tell what they were. He could learn things here, he realized, important things, things that no one else knew. Just one might lead him to all he wanted; something made him sure of that. It might be riches, or every secret of growing things. Knowledge was there; he just had to pick one aspect and follow.

Something brushed his cheek. A tantalizing flower scent drew him from his path. His bond to the *shakkan* tugged at him, making him stop. What was he doing? None of the hints that lured him away felt like Rosethorn.

He opened his hand, inspecting the wisp of her that he'd grabbed when they started to fall. Now he stood in his own skin, or something that felt enough like it to be comfortable. His feet—bare, as they'd been for most of his life—pressed flat gray cobblestones on a gray street in a gray city. There were no windows in the towering citadels all around him, no doors. There wasn't a hint of green anywhere he looked, and no other people. He did see other streets, hundreds of them. They opened onto the dull avenue where he stood.

How was he supposed to find Rosethorn? Even weeds or hedges or the tiniest bit of moss would know Rosethorn's name and murmur it to him. This gray maze was dead.

Not entirely. Sandry's magical voice was a thin whisper. He could feel her straining to hold onto him. *We aren't dead, which means you aren't.*

He turned. A shining rope stretched to infinity behind him. Groping his back with a hand, he discovered it turned into a web of fibers that entered him in a hundred places. In it he could feel the girls.

I ain't coming back without her, he said regretfully.

We never asked you to, Sandry retorted. *Look at that thread you have in your hand. I bet she's at the other end.*

Briar looked. She was right. Wrapping it around his fingers, he began to follow it.

Something jarred her. Tris looked back to the magical blaze that was Daja. *What's going on?* she demanded. *I don't need any diversions, you know!*

Sorry, Daja said sheepishly. *People are shaking me, trying to make me let go.*

Well, tell them to stop, snapped Tris. *We're busy!*

Sandry murmured to Tris.

Sandry says, tell them if they break our rope, they'll lose us all.

Daja obeyed. The jarring stopped.

Better, said Tris. She renewed her grip on Sandry and on Daja, and waited.

He walked forever. Every time he stopped, to catch his breath or to massage his aching feet, visions and sounds flowed over him, trying to distract him. They would make him let go—he would never see Rosethorn or the girls again.

"Tempt somebody else," he growled.

He might have thought he was on a giant wheel, walking around and around inside it without getting anywhere, except that the ball of thread from Rosethorn got bigger in his hands. When it was the size of a peach, and he'd found a blister on his right foot, he noticed something else: a sprout of grass between cobblestones.

He knelt and brushed it with his fingertips. "Am I ever glad to see *you*," he told it. Getting up, he walked on. He saw another blade of grass, then a tuft of it. Touching the slender leaves, he realized the fluffs of temptation had left him after he greeted that first grass shoot.

"Dunno if that's good or bad," he admitted, and trudged on.

Here was a buttercup, its yellow so vivid in all that gray rock that it had the effect of a shout. Here was a clump of moss. He covered it with his palm for a moment, refreshed by that velvet coolness on his skin. He moved on, the ball in his hands the size of a melon.

His feet were bleeding when he found a patch of purple and violet crocuses that had thrust cobblestones from the road. He began to run. Crocuses were Rosethorn's favorite spring flower: she had talked about their arrival for a month.

Running got harder. The plants were rioting, overturning stones, leaving holes for an unwary boy to wrench his ankle if he didn't look sharp. The gray buildings shrank as he found more living things. Finally they vanished altogether. So too did the cobblestone road, giving way to a broad carpet of lush grass. It lay before a stretch of wrought-iron fence nearly fifteen feet high.

He put down the ball of thread. Now it moved on its own, rolling itself up as it traveled. It didn't have far to go: there was an open gate in the fence. Inside stood Rosethorn, looking over her new domain.

Briar hesitated. He couldn't see her face, but he knew the set of her back, the will in those hands planted so firmly on her hips. Ahead of her lay a vast garden in chaos. Trees, bushes, and flowers did battle with weeds, and lost. A fountain bubbled as if it gasped for life, its spouts clogged with moss, its drains stopped with dead leaves. Some type of climbing vine Briar had never seen before had laid claim to everything to his left. It was a gardener's dream, a mess that would take months, even years, to return to its proper glory.

His fingers itched, too. Like his teacher, he did enjoy a challenge.

Not this *challenge!* cried Sandry. She strained to hold onto him. *There are challenges back home, for both of you!*

The ball of thread rolled to Rosethorn's feet and vanished into her. Startled, she turned and saw Briar.

Her eyebrows came together with a nearly audible click; her red mouth pursed. She looked better— healthier, more alive—than she had in weeks. "Absolutely not," she said firmly. "Turn right back around. Girls," she called, "bring him in!"

"Nope," he informed her. "Not without you."

"Don't be absurd," she snapped. "You have a long life in store."

"So do you," he replied stubbornly.

246

"I did good work, I did important work, and now it's over. Perhaps I didn't want it this way and this soon, but you can see there's another lifetime's worth of labor here." She looked over her shoulder at that garden, which so clearly needed someone very good to look after it. Cleaned up properly, it would be magnificent.

"I don't care," Briar said flatly. "We don't belong here. We belong with the girls and Little Bear. And Niko, and Frostpine," he added, seeing her flinch at each name, knowing it gave her pain to hear them, and not caring. She wanted to leave him! "—and—yes, Crane! You'd be leaving him behind. What of Lark? Her most of all—tell me that don't matter to you."

Rosethorn looked down, her mouth working.

"Come home," whispered Briar.

She came over and hugged him fiercely, then let him go. Briar trembled. She *looked* solid enough, but she felt transparent. If a whisper had a body, that was what he'd embraced. "I'm tired," she told him softly. "Tired to the bone. I want to rest."

"Rest at *home*," he repeated stubbornly.

"Briar, it's my time, and it isn't yours. Go back to the girls. You'll break their hearts if you get lost here." She turned to pick up a basket and shears he hadn't seen in the grass before that moment.

"You're breaking *my* heart," he said quietly.

She straightened, her back to him. "I can't go back," she said patiently. "It will hurt."

"'Scuze me for thinking it's worth it to pick up a few ouches!" he cried. She was not coming back for any street rat. Briar had playmates to look after him. Briar didn't need a great plant-mage who kept his heart in her pocket. "'Scuze me for thinking maybe you liked me enough to want to come home!"

"I like you, boy," she said gruffly. "I love you. And I am dead. That's that."

He took a breath. Here was the end of the debate. She wouldn't change her mind, not now. Already he could feel Sandry's grip on him fray. They were never supposed to have been able to do this in the first place.

"Fine," he said. He turned, wrapping Sandry's ties to him around his waist. A knife had appeared in the grass by his feet. Had the garden appeared for Rosethorn in this same convenient way? the boy wondered. He scooped the knife up one-handed and began to gather the threads into a rope he could cut.

Rosethorn was always suspicious when he agreed with her. She turned. "What's fine?"

"This. Here." It was harder to gather the threads of his connection to Sandry than he'd expected. She fought, commanding the hair-fine strands to twitch from his grasp. Briar struggled with them—with her. With Daja, feeding the strength of stone to her, and Tris, adding lightning, and the *shakkan* its terrible, unmoving calm, an old tree's patience. "I'll stay here and help." He cast a look at the overgrown park. The vine that covered that side of the garden had the nasty look of something that would throw out new shoots as the old ones were clipped off. "You'll need it."

"Absolutely not!" cried Rosethorn. "You are going home. The girls—"

"They'll miss me, and I'm sorry for that, but they got their teachers, and Lark to make a home. They'll manage. I can't. I'm staying." He began to saw at the fibers, cutting them handful by handful.

The girls argued furiously, refusing to accept his choice. Daja and Tris passed still more of their strength to Sandry. The *shakkan* did not argue. It could only wait.

"Stop fussing!" Briar ordered his friends. "You know why I'm doing this, so let me do it!"

A surge of fresh magic boiled down the tie that bound him to them as he fought to cut the last of it. It wrapped around him like a loop of rope and held him fast.

"Idiots," Rosethorn said, pale and frightened now. "You'll all die—"

Briar gave up trying to reason with them. He sat. The final loop of magic popped over his head as if he'd been oiled. Sandry shrieked in fury and hurled a fine thread around his wrist before they lost him. The thread strained.

"I stay," Briar told Rosethorn. "With you."

With a sigh, Rosethorn dropped the shears and basket, then knelt, folding her arms around him. "You will regret this for the rest of your life," she whispered. "I'm going to see to it."

He wrapped his hands firmly around her wrists, in case she changed her mind abruptly. "I know," he said cheerfully. To the girls he said, "Reel us in."

"Don't you *ever* do that again!"

That was Lark, he thought sleepily. Only why was Lark upset? She was shouting.

He yawned and sat up. His right hand was cramping fiercely. He looked for the answer and saw that he still clutched Rosethorn's hand.

"Rosethorn!" he cried, trying to get up. He was on the floor, and the bed was in his way. "Rosethorn!"

Somehow he got his legs under him and rose to his knees, all the while still gripping her fingers. If he let go, he would lose her. He was a little fuzzy just now, but he remembered that much perfectly.

Rosethorn opened her eyes and coughed. She continued to cough, trying to yank her hand free so she might cover her mouth. On the other side of her bed a woman in a gold-bordered blue habit helped Rosethorn to sit and gave her something to drink. Rosethorn gulped frantically, spraying water from the sides of her mouth. Her coughing eased; she lay back, gasping.

She was alive, then. He could let go.

That was easier thought than done. The cramps in his fingers made it necessary to pry them open, one at a time. When he finally let Rosethorn go, she drew her hand away.

Moonstream—the woman in the gold-bordered habit—regarded Briar, an odd look in her dark eyes. She reached across the bed, cupping his cheek in a hand that smelled faintly like cinnamon, and pursed her plum-colored lips. Magic flowed like cool mist through him, spreading to fill his corners. In the wake of that mist he felt calmer, more solid. More alive.

At last the Dedicate Superior of Winding Circle drew her hand away. Briar looked around. The girls sat between him and the door, looking as rumpled and shocked as he felt. Lark was on her knees beside Sandry, holding the girl tight.

"I am very upset with all of you!" she said, glaring at Briar. "You deliberately disobeyed me!" Her words notwithstanding, she kissed the top of Sandry's head.

"Your eyes are all wet," murmured Tris, reaching up to brush the damp from Lark's cheeks. The distance between them was too great, and Tris seemed too weak to get up.

Niko stood in the doorway, leaning against the frame. His eyes were huge with shock. When he smoothed his mustache, Briar could see he was trembling.

"We're all right, Niko," Sandry assured him. "We're just a little tired."

"Just a bit," Daja mumbled. She dragged her knees up so she could rest her head on them.

Briar remembered something important. "Pneumonia," he told Moonstream hurriedly. "She has pneumonia and she's gonna die—"

"Calm down," Moonstream told him. "I'll see to it." She laid one of her palms on the pulse in Rosethorn's neck.

Silver glimmered and faded. Moonstream looked at Rosethorn, whose eyes met hers. "Well," the Dedicate Superior remarked, taking her hand from Rosethorn's throat. "You *had* pneumonia. Your lungs are perfectly clear now."

"Maybe we burned it out?" Tris inquired, her voice rasping. "Things were—complicated." She removed her spectacles and rubbed her eyes.

"What happened to Sealwort?" Daja asked, furious. "He never came!"

"Leave Sealwort to me," replied Lark, her eyes cold. "He probably said he'd come just to get rid of me."

"*I* will talk to Sealwort," Moonstream said firmly. "I'd prefer if everything that happened today were kept as quiet as possible, if you don't mind."

Rosethorn tugged weakly at Moonstream's sleeve and opened her mouth. No sound came out. She gasped, and tried again. Only garbled sounds without sense emerged. Scrambling, the three girls crowded around the bed.

"She can't talk?" demanded Briar, frightened. "Why can't she? Did we do something? Did I do something?" She had a seizure—how long had she gone

252

without breathing? Was she to spend her life unable to speak?

Rosethorn gripped his arm.

Calm down, she said, her magic every bit as weak as her arms. *I choked, didn't I?*

"She choked," Briar said pleadingly to Moonstream. "She turned blue."

Once again Moonstream rested a hand against the pulse in Rosethorn's throat. Since Rosethorn still held onto him, Briar felt that drift of mist that was Moonstream's power in motion. It spread into Rosethorn's brain, idly questing as a real fog might hunt for a door to fit into.

"A small part of her mind died when she stopped breathing," Moonstream told her audience. "Very small. She only needs to learn how to speak again, and she will be her old self." The mist drew back into Moonstream, and she lowered her hand. "They must have grabbed you at the very moment you passed on."

Rosethorn tugged at Moonstream's arm and pointed firmly at Briar.

"Briar grabbed you," Moonstream said, understanding. She held Briar's eyes with hers. "You were warned about what could happen. What should have happened."

All four young people nodded. Sandry, an obedient girl, was shamefaced. Daja shrugged; Tris fiddled with her spectacles. Briar met Moonstream's calm brown gaze with defiance. He would do it again.

Moonstream shook her head, then looked at Niko and Lark. "It would be a very good idea if no one ever talked about this," she said quietly. "A *very* good idea. This—" She motioned to Rosethorn, who nodded. "This has never happened. I don't know how it *did* happen, and I don't *want* to know."

Briar and the girls exchanged looks. *They* knew.

Two months later, after the noon meal, the four retired to their favorite lounging place, the roof of Discipline. Cushioned by fragrant thatch they'd all helped to replace three weeks before, they draped themselves around the chimney and watched clouds. Around them was the great bowl that encompassed the temple city, with the Hub tower as its axle. Shriek the starling perched on top of the cold chimney, taunting other starlings as they flew by. If the four glanced into the hatchway that led into the house, they could see Little Bear curled up on the attic floor, mournfully awaiting their return. Lark was in her workroom. They'd left Rosethorn at the table, writing a letter.

Steps sounded on wood; the ladder creaked. Briar and Daja, just on the other side of the peak of the roof, crawled up to see who was coming.

A gray-and-black head poked up through the opening in the thatch. "Bless me, I don't see how you keep from breaking your necks," remarked Niko. "I would be scared to death." Climbing a little more, he

254

sat on the edge of the opening, trying not to look over the roof's edge. Clothed with his usual elegance, he was out of place on the thatch. Briar chuckled, looking at him.

"The view is good from up here," Daja explained drowsily as she folded herself over the peak. "And it's nice and warm."

"I'm getting freckles," commented Tris, leaning on the chimney.

"Do you know what today is?" Sandry asked them.

"My birthday?" asked Briar drily. She pestered him about that still.

"If you want it," Sandry replied. "But I was actually thinking it was *our* birthday, in a manner of speaking."

They all looked at her, even Niko, unsure of what she meant.

"A year ago today, Tris and I came to Discipline." Sandry beamed at them all. "It was the first time the four of us were together."

Briar whistled. "Doesn't seem that long ago."

"It does and it doesn't," remarked Daja. Looking at her three friends, she shook her head. "I never expected things to turn out as they have."

"Who could?" Tris inquired. "We didn't know we had magic, for one thing."

"Niko did," replied Daja with a glance at the man. "Just like you knew where we were, when no one else did—"

"Or no one else cared," murmured Briar.

Niko surveyed each of them. "Things didn't turn out as I expected, either," he admitted.

"What *did* you expect?" Sandry asked, curious.

Niko's smile was wry. "I expected to pick up some young mages, find them teachers, and go on my way. I never thought to endure earthquakes, pirates, forest fires, and plagues with them, or to be forced to revise my knowledge of how magic is shaped. I had forgotten that there is never a point at which we stop learning, or needing to learn. You remind me of that every day—whether I wish such a reminder or not."

Sandry reached over to pat his hand. "You're doing very well," she said in her most Larkish manner. She glanced below and got to her feet. "Oh, look," she cried, pointing toward the north gate. "It's Uncle. We're going riding, and I haven't changed yet!" She waved gleefully to a distant company of riders. Their leader waved back to her.

Niko shuddered. "Don't jump around like that," he said, shifting so he could climb down the ladder into the house. "It makes me nervous. Coming, Tris?"

"Coming," she replied, getting up. She followed Sandry inside.

"Got to go," Daja said, glancing at the Hub clock. "Frostpine wants to clean the forge this afternoon."

Briar smirked. "Better wash before you come home," he advised.

"I mean to," she said, and left him in possession of the roof.

256

The Hub clock banged out the second hour of the afternoon. The midday rest period was over. Briar stared at clouds and thought of birthdays. He really ought to decide on one. After long meditation, he'd decided he looked forward to having a birthday. For one thing, it would mean a cake. How could he turn down extra food?

Today?

No. Like she'd said, today was a birthday for them, for that lumpy circle of thread Sandry was forever carrying about.

He'd decided against Midsummer. That was Rosethorn's, even if she did hide it in the temple-wide celebration of the summer solstice. It had occurred to him that he ought to have a day that was his, to mark how far he'd come, and who he had been. It should be a day with meaning for both Roach and Briar, for the street rat and the mage. It ought to be a green day: one of Roach's calmest memories was of a patch of moss in a dank jail cell, a bit of comfort where he'd expected none. It wasn't the day that a Bag calling himself Niklaren Goldeye bought Roach free of the Hajra docks; Niko had then dragged Roach all the way to Emelan and Winding Circle, even if he called that boy the brand-new name of Briar Moss. Briar had also considered the day he stole the *shakkan*, and discarded it, as well as a handful of others.

The day that had changed him for all time, that

had marked the turning from Roach to Briar, had been a day he'd come to this same roof. He'd been lazing, watching clouds, and thinking of nothing, when his contemplation had been interrupted. . . .

"Come on, boy!" a gleeful voice cried from the garden below. "You're wasting daylight!"

It was the same voice that called to him now. He got to his feet with a sigh, but the truth was, he didn't want to waste the light either. You never knew when you'd need it and not have it.

"What's the chore today?" he yelled down to Rosethorn.

"Weeding!" she called back. "It's summer, isn't it? So it's always weeding!"

Her speech was a little slurred and might always be. Still, she could speak clearly. Better yet, her mind was as sharp as ever.

She had called to him to come down and work in her garden the day after his arrival at Discipline, the twentieth day of Goose Moon—which was tomorrow. The girls would be vexed at getting so little time to prepare, but they would adjust. They would know, as he did, that his life began when Rosethorn had invited him into her world.

"Briar!" she called.

"It ain't running away without us!" he yelled in reply, and climbed back into the house.

Start at the beginning, and see how the magic unfolds...

The Circle Opens Quartet

- ❑ 0-590-39605-6 The Circle Opens #1: Magic Steps $5.99 US
- ❑ 0-590-39643-9 The Circle Opens #2: Street Magic $5.99 US
- ❑ 0-590-39656-0 The Circle Opens #3: Cold Fire $5.99 US
- ❑ 0-590-39696-X The Circle Opens #4: Shatterglass $5.99 US

Fresh New Look!

The Circle of Magic Quartet

- ❑ 0-590-55408-5 Circle of Magic #1: Sandry's Book $5.99 US
- ❑ 0-590-55409-3 Circle of Magic #2: Tris's Book $5.99 US
- ❑ 0-590-55410-7 Circle of Magic #3: Daja's Book $5.99 US
- ❑ 0-590-55411-5 Circle of Magic #4: Briar's Book $5.99 US

Available wherever you buy books, or use this order form.

Scholastic Inc., P.O. Box 7502, Jefferson City, MO 65102

Please send me the books I have checked above. I am enclosing $_____ (please add $2.00 to cover shipping and handling). Send check or money order—no cash or C.O.D.s please.

Name_____Age_____

Address_____

City_____State/Zip_____

Please allow four to six weeks for delivery. Offer good in the U.S. only. Sorry, mail orders are not available to residents of Canada. Prices subject to change.

■SCHOLASTIC

COMOT

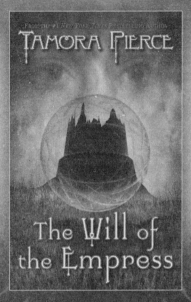

Tamora Pierce says she first got the idea for the Circle of Magic books by watching her mother and sister do needlework. "Seeing them knit, quilt, and crochet in the evenings, I often thought—as I eyed my two left hands—that what I witnessed was magic in our real world, the magic of turning thread and cloth into beautiful, useful things with little fuss or ceremony. That notion lodged in my brain. For years I fiddled with the concept of crafts magic, including a play, a short story, and mentions in a book that all dealt with thread magic.

"At the same time I was conducting those experiments, I became friends with an artist jeweler who, over the course of his long career, had turned his hand not only to weaving, sewing, and embroidery, but also to architecture, woodworking, pottery, glassblowing, and the smithing of all kinds of metals. Our friendship broadened my conception of magic expressed in crafts, while my initial fascination with magic worked in thread gave me a place to start. Offered the chance by Scholastic to create a new magical universe, I decided to get serious about crafts and their power, both real and imagined."

Tamora Pierce was born in western Pennsylvania, has lived in various states across the country, and currently resides in New York City with her husband. A graduate of the University of Pennsylvania, she has studied social work, film, and psychology. She has worked as head writer for a radio production company, martial arts movie reviewer, housemother in a group home, literary agent's assistant, and investment banking secretary. Today she is a full-time writer.

Ms. Pierce began to write at the age of eleven. Her first two fantasy cycles, The Song of the Lioness and The Immortals, are very popular with young readers and have won many honors. The Circle of Magic quartet—including *Sandry's Book*, *Tris's Book*, *Daja's Book*, and *Briar's Book*— has been hailed by reviewers as "gripping adventure" (*School Library Journal*) and "a rich and satisfying read" (*Kirkus Reviews*). Upcoming are four more books, called The Circle Opens, which will feature some characters familiar from the Circle of Magic as well as many new ones.